FTB Presents: Irrational Fears

An Anthology

FTB Press

Chandler, AZ USA

Irrational Fears

FTB Press, LLC.

Chandler, AZ USA

Printed in the USA.

ISBN-13: 978-0692498125

ISBN-10: 0692498125

This book is a work of fiction. Stories and characters are a product of the individual author's imagination and any resemblance to any actual persons, living or dead is purely coincidental.

Irrational Fears

Irrational Fears

Table of Contents:

Irrational Fears

Introduction...

From time to time, I enjoy putting in my headphones, listening to the Foo Fighters and going for a run along this canal by my house. It has a nice, flat, dirt path, and the water, although it sometimes smells like old socks, I find peaceful when jogging. That is until one day when this roadrunner zoomed past me...I stopped in my tracks and paused the music. This was a new feeling. A sudden fear. I looked around. I knew there had to be a Wile E. Coyote somewhere. Behind the power pole? Maybe in a nearby bush? Or perhaps floating in an Acme helium balloon? That speedy little bird was running for a reason. He was about to experience the shock and awe of a hailstorm of Acme safes and anvils raining from the sky.

My fine feathered friend runs fast and I needed to catch up and return to the safety of my home. My only thought when I got home? I hope no one spills any black paint. Where do you go when you fall in that hole?

The ridiculous experience of mine is the inspiration for the first book from FTB Press, Irrational Fears. The book is a collection of works from a talented and diverse group of international writers. As a press, we hope to share the voice of new, emerging, and established writers with a shared community of readers. You have a choice of where to spend your hard-earned dollars and may have sacrificed an iced latte to buy this book and for that, we thank you. Please enjoy, Irrational Fears.

Cheers,

Scott Lange

FTB Press Founder

Irrational Fears

Darkness, My Demon

By Essel Pratt

Fear. For some it is the unknown waiting within the shadowy places inside our rooms on the darkest nights. For others it is the banshee calls whistling upon the winds outside our drafty bedroom windows. Still, for others, fear is the feeling of knowing there is something in our presence that we cannot see, touch, or smell, but can feel staring at us from somewhere out of sight. Still many more believe fear to be nothing more than an archaic defense mechanism that is to be ignored until forgotten. Regardless of how we envision it, fear does not work alone; she has many allies at her beckon.

While I lie here in my bed, with the blankets wrapped around my head, breathing my warm recycled breath within my personal cocoon, I try to ignore my fear and mimic the brave souls that can shove it off so easily. I am a grown ass man, yet I hide here shivering within the confines of my anxiety. My deep breathes further my panic as I dread the creature in the corner, behind the door, believing it is blind to my camouflage but privy to my presence by the sounds I unwillingly make. I try to calm my nerves and think of something besides the invisible reaper that watches over my body. The cold sweat that has formed on my upper lip mocks my childish terror and I begin to weep.

Disappointed in myself, I muster the courage to peek out from the ripped corner of my sanctuary, only to stare darkness in the eye. The creature that I fear is not visible in my narrow view of the room, yet I can feel him staring at me, no through me, through my soul. My heart begins to palpitate rapidly again, sending sharp pains through my chest. I have to stop the panic, so I reach for the plastic pill bottle on my nightstand. My fingers flutter with nerves as I grasp for the cylindrical container, spilling it and the Xanax to the floor.

My nerves are causing the pains to contract within my chest. I need to get my pills so I can relax, but the fear in my mind is too great. I pull the covers from my head and glance around the room. The reaper is nowhere to be found. He must be under my bed now, with the bottle and scattered pills. The thought of him mocking me from below does little to comfort me any further. Peeking over the edge of my bed, the little white pills contrast against the hand-heaved oaken floors. They are within an arm's reach away, but I cannot find the strength to extend my arm to their resting place.

I hear a noise in the corner, behind the door. I turn my head quickly, straining a muscle or something; the pain does not null the sharpness in my chest. I struggle to find my cell phone on the table. It vibrated as a text message signaled its arrival, making it easier to find in the darkness. With it safely in my grip, I fumble through the multitude of useless apps to find the one that turns the camera flash into a flashlight.

With newfound courage, which can only be attributed to my cellular saving grace, I scan the room for that which should not be present. I discover the source of noise near the entry was nothing more than the ceiling mounted heat vent pushing the door slightly closed as the warm air forced through the outlet. I try to inhale three more deep breathes to assist in relieving my anxiety induced chest pains. Yet still, in the back of my mind I know that I am not alone in the room.

Despite my inability to cope with the fear that is surging through me, I force myself to reach for the pills. I only need one to calm me. My arm is still shaky, I am not sure if it is from terror or from the anxiety, but it makes picking up the medication a difficult task. However, being persistent, I manage to grab two of the pills and quickly shove them in my mouth. With no water nearby, and the incapability to swallow pills without it, I quickly chew them and force the powdery mess down my throat. The taste nearly makes me gag, but the medicine calms me down. The chest pains begin to diminish.

Feeling better, I emerge from my blanket cocoon and place my feet upon the cold floor. A loose nail pushes against my heel. I must remember to pound it flush in the morning. My hands caress my face, as they balance upon my still shaky knees. Again, I take two deep breathes to clear my head. On the third breath, I feel something brush against my foot; this foot rests on top of the nail. I desperately slid my foot away from the assailant, scraping a chasm of skin from my cracked heel. The pain is minimal, but blood is pouring from the wound at a decent drip.

Upset with myself for getting so worked up, I limp to the bathroom, careful not to soil the throw rugs with my crimson excretion. It only takes a second to fumble for the switch before illuminating my way to the medicine cabinet. Once my eyes adjust, I shouldn't have looked directly at the lights when I turned them on; I fumble through the cabinet for a couple of loose Band-Aids. Opening one side of the mirrored double door I noticed something moving behind me in the reflection. I turn to get a better glimpse, but nothing is there. I can feel my anxiety rising once again.

To take my mind off the fear, I sit upon the commode and clean the bloody mess from my foot with a nearby washcloth. The wound is not as bad as it looks and will not require stitches, so I affix the Band-Aids. All the while, I glance into my dark bedroom searching for the faceless nuisance that has taunted me in the dark. I know I am not insane. I know there is no need to fear the dark. Yet something haunts me, or maybe it taunts me, within the shadows.

The pills have worked well. My heartbeat has returned to normal and the pains in my chest are nothing more than a memory. I hate those pains. Whenever they assault me, I think the worst. The fear of a heart attack while I am alone with no one to call only increases the panic attack. There are times the pills do not work and hours go by before I finally calm enough to move on with my life. Then there are the times like tonight when the nefarious reaper stalks me in the realm between reality and sanity. I don't know why he has chosen me, nor do I know if he acts alone. He is good at his job; I know that he works alongside my fears.

The fluorescent hum of the light above me is comforting, as is the artificial glow. I contemplate sleeping in the tub, with the light on. Then I remember that I am a man, not a child. I start to sob like a child, wondering why I feel this way. As a child, I was never this bad. I was brave and vigilant against the monsters that stalked me in the dark. I knew they were there hiding in my closet and under my bed. Always stalking. Always plotting. Sometimes they spoke to me, but I wouldn't listen.

Now that I think of it, when the voices stopped is when fear took control of my life. Their silence made me nervous. I no longer knew where they were hiding or what they were thinking. Maybe they are getting their revenge on me now, in my adult life, mocking me with each assault. There are shadowy figures mocking me in my peripheral and taunting me with the unknown.

I have not slept much in recent nights. Fatigue is consuming my sanity. I know that I must sleep, but the bedroom is so dark. I do not know what lies in wait for me, so I am still sitting upon my porcelain throne, breathing rhythmically, inhaling deeply, and building the courage to run to my bed and hide within the safety of my blankets. I am not yet brave enough, so I stare into the darkness.

In the spot between my bed and the floor, I can see a faint mass of movement. I rub my eyes to see if they are playing tricks on me once again, but the figure is still there. I can feel the sweat bead upon my brow as a shiny set of eyes peers at me. Their yellow glow alerts me of their steady glare. My heart is beating fast again. There is pain in my chest and my anxiety is getting the best of me.

I stand to move closer to the door so I can shut it, sealing myself away from the demon that stalks me. My arm is numb. I cannot force the limb to obey my mind's orders. Tears swell in my eyes. I see the eyes meandering closer to me, and the pain in my chest intensifies beyond any that I have ever felt before. The world goes black and I feel my body slam upon the tile floor.

* * *

I find myself sitting upon the toilet once again, staring down upon my corpse. Upon my chest, a fluffy black kitten kneads my flesh as it tries to create a comforting cushion to rest. It is shivering, maybe from the chill of my body. I wonder how it got in my bedroom until the fluttering curtains reveal that I left the window open at some point. The kitten must have come in through there.

I switch my focus back to my body and realize I am no longer afraid or in pain. I actually feel good for once. I am not tired, but I decide to lie down anyway. My body is large, but I seem to float over it as I traverse my way to the bed. I don't bother covering up. I just lie down upon the heavy comforter and close my eyes. Darkness envelops me and the world disappears.

I am no longer fearful.

Gasoline

By Wayne Via

I've always dreaded the day when I'd have to explain my extreme fear of gasoline to a stranger. It's not the golden color of the liquid, or the cool sensation when it touches my skin. It's always been the smell that brings back the memories, and the memories that bring back the terror. Even the thought of visiting a gas station frightens me. Over the past couple of years, I've always been able to find at least one old friend or acquaintance willing to drive to the gas station and fill up my car, but as time passed, the list of willing volunteers has gotten shorter and shorter. This afternoon, I find myself with a nearly empty tank of gas, a long list of errands, and no one willing to help.

After spending the morning calling and listening to excuses, I found myself standing at the front window of my home, contemplating which neighbor might be willing to help. I hesitated to approach any of them until I saw Bob pulling into his driveway.

Bob was new to our small, rural neighborhood. He was young and single. I doubt he'd met many of the neighbors, much less heard all the gossip from years gone by He was nice enough to fill my tank once before after I lied, telling him I'd broken my finger.

I grabbed my keys and raced across the street. I stood next to his car, patiently waiting and watching as he fiddled with his phone. I was pretty sure he saw me, but I walked to the front of the car and waved, just to make sure. Finally, he opened the car door.

"Bob, I need a favor. My car's almost out of gas and I was hoping...."

"I'm sorry, Earl," he said holding up his hand, barely glancing in my direction. "I've got too many things to do today. You'll just have to find someone else to fetch your gas." He started walking towards his front door. I could hear the car doors lock behind me as I followed him.

"Please, Bob, I'd do it myself if I could."

"You don't look handicapped to me." He said as he unlocked his front door and went inside. The door was swinging shut when I stuck my foot beside the jamb.

"Sometimes the most painful wounds aren't visible." I pleaded. "Please, give me a few minutes to explain. I'll tell you a story you won't forget."

The front door slowly began to open. Curiosity had won him over.

"All right, come on in." Bob said as he turned and walked toward the back of the house.

I shut the door and followed close behind him. He was much taller than me, and it was hard for me to keep up. We passed through an empty living room and into the den. It was definitely the home of a bachelor. The only furniture in the den was a black leather chair, a TV, and three bar stools along the counter that divided the kitchen from the den.

"Can I get you something?" He asked as he walked into the kitchen.

"No, I'm fine."

Bob motioned for me to sit at the counter facing the kitchen. I took a seat and watched as he grabbed a beer from the refrigerator, opened it, and took a long drink. Finally, leaning his back against the sink he turned his attention to me.

"Okay, now what's your story?" He asked.

I stared at the counter for a few seconds. How do I describe the most painful day of my life to a person I don't even know?

"Bob, you know where the stop sign is down on Hampton Road?"

He nodded his head.

"Well, that stop sign didn't use to be there, not until after my wife..."

"Wife?" Bob replied, as he sat his beer on the counter. "I didn't know you were married."

"I'll get to that. As I was going to say, that used to be a blind intersection. The two roads simply merged together. Sometimes I'd be driving down the hill after work and people would just pull out in front of me. It was as if I wasn't even there. I don't know how many times I had to slam on my brakes and just hoped I didn't hit them or drive off into the ditch. I'd get home and complain to my wife, Angela, about it all the time, thinking I'd at least get a little sympathy from her."

Bob took another sip.

"I kept asking her to call the police, or complain to the city about how dangerous the intersection was, but she never did. I found out later, she did convince a couple of our neighbors to call, but she never called herself."

"Anyway, I used to mow the lawn every Saturday morning. It was my weekend ritual. Even if we had something else planned, I always cut the grass first. On the day of the accident, I went into the garage as usual, but the lawnmower's tank was bone dry, and so was the gas can. I went back inside and told Angela I was going to run up to the gas station. She said she needed to do her grocery shopping. I offered to take her to the market, but she insisted on driving her own car. She said it was because the market was off in the other direction. Then she made a point of suggesting I pick up an extra can or two of gas so I wouldn't have to run to the station all the time."

Bob finished his beer, set the bottle down hard on the counter, and glanced over at the refrigerator. I could see I was losing his interest.

"When I got to the gas station, I bought two extra plastic gas cans, and filled up all three. I was driving back home down the grade , when right as I got to Hampton Road, a car sped through the intersection and plowed straight into the side of my car. It just came out of nowhere. I couldn't even brace myself for impact."

Bob's attention shifted from the refrigerator, to me.

"The car pushed me into the ditch. My car rolled over and landed on its roof. My head slammed into the side window, knocking me unconscious. When I came to, I was hanging upside down with the seat belt holding me in place. My arms were dangling below my head, resting in a pool of gas."

I paused for a second. My nostrils flared from simply the memory of the fumes.

"It took me a few seconds to realize what had happened. As I hung there helpless, I looked outside the window and I saw my wife, the love of my life, standing motionless beside the car. The gasoline was seeping out through the car window and creating a puddle right outside the door. I'd carelessly placed the gas cans on the floor of the back seat for the short ride home. Now they were below me, lying on their sides, leaking from caps. There was gas everywhere. My clothes were drenched. My nose burned and eyes were stinging. Worst of all, I wasn't sure if it was steam or smoke coming out from under the hood."

"I started screaming for help, hoping and praying my wife would do something before the gas ignited, but she just stood there, frozen in fear. I fought with the seat belt, pushing the release button, tugging and pulling on the belt, but the clasp wouldn't let go. I twisted and turned, trying to squeeze my hips out of the lap belt, but it was just too tight. I was trapped. There was no getting out, and the smell of gas was getting stronger and stronger. I was coughing and choking, fighting for a breath of fresh air. I finally gave up trying."

"I kept looking over at my wife. Why doesn't she do something? Why wasn't she helping me? I'll never forget the look of panic I saw on her face as she stood there. She knew my life was in her hands. The gas was all around us. One spark and the car would be engulfed in flames, probably killing us both. There was nothing I could do about it. It was all up to her. I still don't know if it was fumes or tears that made my eyes water, but I remember wiping them repeatedly so I could look into my beautiful wife's eyes just one more time before our lives went up in smoke."

Bob leaned forward, staring directly in my eyes.

"That day, that morning, those few minutes, changed my life forever." I crossed my arms on the counter and lowered my head, trying to hide my tears. "That's why I can't go back to a gas station. I can't relive that day, I just can't."

Compassion is a hard emotion for men to express, but I knew my story had really touched Bob. He walked over to me and placed his hand on my shoulder.

"How did you get out? Were you burned?" He asked.

I raised my head.

"Oh, there was no fire." I said, wiping my eyes. "Another driver saw my car lying upside down, and ran over to help. He stopped my wife right before she had a chance to ignite the gasoline. He wrestled a cigarette lighter out of her hand and she ran off. He cut me loose from the seatbelt, and then pulled me out of the car. I was really lucky he drove by when he did."

"Wait a minute." Bob looked confused. "So your wife didn't just happen by the scene of the crash? How did she end up outside the car?"

"She drove the car that hit me. I guess she planned the whole thing. She figured all that extra gas would catch fire

21

and burn me to a crisp. At the trial, she claimed it was an accident. She said she was coming back from the grocery store and never saw me coming. She said it was just a coincidence that it was me in the other car. Her lawyer told the jury how the neighbors had complained to the city about that intersection. The only thing he couldn't explain was why my wife was trying to strike a cigarette lighter while I was trapped in a pool of gas. I guess everything didn't go the way she planned."

"What happened to her? Did the police charge her? Is she in jail? "

"Yea, they charged her with attempted murder, but they said with good behavior she'll be out in another year. I guess our love was a bit one-sided, but I still can't believe she wanted me dead. Every time I see her, I ask her why she did it. She never gives me a reason."

"You still keep in touch with her?"

Bob's expression changed from concern to disbelief.

"Of course I do. That's why I need the gas. Today is visiting day and it's a long drive. You've got to understand, I still love her, she's my whole life."

Bob yanked his hand off my shoulder. "I can't believe you came over here to ask me to buy you gas, so that you can go visit the woman who tried to kill you."

I stood up, shaking my head.

"I shouldn't have told you that story. I didn't think a bachelor like you would understand. My old friends, they knew how much I loved her. I just wish they wouldn't have stopped helping me. I need them now more than ever."

"They weren't helping you. The best way for them to help you is to make you face the fact that your wife must have hated you so much she'd rather see you dead than have to spend another day with you. You need help alright, but it's not with pumping your gas."

We stood there staring at each other for a few seconds, and then Bob walked to the front door. He threw it open and looked back at me. "Go home, Earl, and see if you can find a backbone somewhere along the way."

I went outside, and heard the door slam behind me. As I walked home, I started thinking about what Bob had said. I thought about the phone calls I made that morning. How they also ended with a slam. I stopped to look at my empty house. I reached into my pocket, pulled out my car keys, and walked to my car. I knew Bob was right. I have to overcome my fears if I ever want to get on with my life. I have to man up and get my own damn gas. I must. Angela would be so disappointed if I didn't show up today.

Crazy 8

By Lance Hyden

Who doesn't like to let off a little steam after a long work week? My boy Rick sure as hell does. He's out there right now cutting a rug with every lady that's willing and able. I, however, just like to chill at the bar and watch the hunnies walk by at The Lucky Seven Nightclub. He's the dancer and partier and I'm the talker and listener—this combo has worked for years. Tonight the club has no shortage of two o'clock beauty queens to take home, or at the very least, a parking lot blowjob. It's just one of the perks of having a jet black 2015 Ford Mustang with dark tinted windows.

Rick approaches the bar, sweating and smiling, taking a break from his endless dancing. He grabs his glass of Vodka and Red Bull to quench his thirst. Everyone knows this drink as the Raging Bull. Rick likes to rename things his own way, so he calls his favorite party drink The Russian Matador. After he downs his beverage he whips out his cell phone and yells out, "Hey bro, let's take a solitary." Yeah, that's a selfie. That'll be on his Facebook page, Twitter feed, and Instagram within the next two minutes. Rick's a social networking freak. I'm sorry, I mean digital community freak.

That's when a blond and red headed Betty walk up to the bar. A Betty is a hot chick, a Wilma is a doable chick, and a Dino is, well, you get the picture. Rick insists that one of these fine ladies accompany him to the dance floor. He has confidence, good looks, style, and is very persuasive. She takes his hand and away they go. This leaves me alone with the other beautiful creature that walked into our lives. "Well that was quick." I say to break the silence.

"Not really, she wanted to meet him." She explained. So I guess it wasn't his persuasion this time, just his other three attributes.

The rest of the night, we engaged in lengthy conversation about nothing and everything. Before we realized it, the club was closing, nearly empty, and Rick and his Betty had disappeared. This was the first time I spent the entire night talking to one girl and didn't think about getting her into my car. Hell, usually by now, I have two or three women's digits and I'd be leaving with another. I don't dare offer her a ride home or ask for one of those parking lot specials, this chick is too cool.

We walk to her car, an ordinary 2010 Toyota Camry. That's when I realized that this whole time we never introduced ourselves. "Hey, I never got your name. I'm Bryan." I said with a nervous laugh. Betty, we'll call her for the moment, opened her car door and got in without saying anything. My first thought was *what the fuck?* She reached into a bag on the passenger seat and pulled out a notebook and pen.

I stood there in silence while she wrote something down. She tore out the piece of paper, folded it up, and handed to me. "Here you go Bryan, call me." She shut her car door, started the engine, and drove off.

Damn, not even a hug? Heartless witch! I think I'm in love. I took the folded piece of enchantment and put it in my pocket without looking at it. I want to wait until I get home to learn this sexy siren's name.

The clock on my stove reads 2:37am. I throw my keys on the counter and grab a beer out of the refrigerator. That's when I get a Snap Chat from Rick; he's banging his Betty doggy style. Hmm, nice tramp stamp of a heart and some swirly design. I open my beer, sit on the couch, and turn on Sports Center. They're talking about LeBron James again. When aren't they? I quickly turn to something other than the LeBron Channel. At this point, it's just noise, there's something else I'd rather look at.

Now it's time to see what this wonderful sorceress' name is. I anxiously unfold the college ruled piece of notebook paper. In beautiful handwriting she wrote, Jo X1X-555-0XXX call me. While staring at the written information, an intense panic attack ensues. I quickly throw the paper down and take deep breathes to calm down. I'm not going to sleep very well tonight and it's too late at night to call my sponsor. I'm lucky I am meeting with my support group tomorrow morning. Shit, only six hours away, I have to try to get some sleep.

It's early, but the room's full. I see all the regulars and some newbies. Miguel my sponsor is here. We make eye contact and he walks my way. "Hey bro, I almost had to call you at 2:30 last night because of this." I hand him the piece of paper.

"Damn Man, look at all those eights. You should've called." He hands the paper back. His concern about the amount of Xs on that piece of paper is the reason why I'm here. I suffer from Octophobia, the fear of the figure X.

We take our seats, in what I like to call the circle of freaks. The session begins. JoAnn, the group's therapist, enters and sits down. "Let's get started. Who wants to be first?" she asks. The regulars consist of John, three seats to my left, who has Meteorophobia. Meteors freak him out. Every couple of minutes he walks over to the window and looks up towards the sky. Sitting by himself is Smelly Steve; he suffers from Ablutophobia, the fear of washing or bathing. Across from me is the lovely Alison, who's overcome by Hominophobia, the fear of men. I tried to hit on her the first day and she flipped out and started screaming. I haven't said a word to her since. The king of the freaks has to go to Charlie sitting to my right. Charlie's diagnosis is Arachibutyrophobia, the fear of peanut butter sticking to the roof of your mouth. His mother would only feed him peanut butter for every meal from age three to seven. Not even the good kind, like creamy Skippy, he was fed generic chunky style store brands.

"I'll start JoAnn." Charlie jumps right in. "I have some great news. The woman I met a couple weeks ago has invited me for a weekend getaway." The group claps, but I don't. I just sit and wonder if that woman knows about his phobia. Most of us don't share our fears with anyone outside of these walls. Irrational fears can be embarrassing. It took me years before I could find help with a support group. Thoughts of Bobbie Jo keep me from participating.

Oh great! Artic Brad speaks up. Everybody hates when he speaks. He supports my theory that if you're in a group of five or more people that you don't know, there's always that one annoying person that never stops talking or asks dumb fucking questions. Brad! You have Chionophobia. The fear of snow... and you live in L.A., Talk about an irrational fear. What a moron. I want to get through this meeting so I can call Bobbie Jo.

Rick thinks that waiting three days to call a Betty is a perfect time. If you're too early then you come across as desperate and if you're too late then she'll lose interest. He dials Bobbie Jo's number for me because I can't handle all those Xs. I'll have him save her number in my phone so I don't have to touch that dreaded TUV key every time I want to call her. The phone is ringing and Rick hands it back to me. Wow, my heart is racing with nerves and excitement. This has never happened before when calling a Betty, Wilma, or a Dino. Well, I've never called a Dino. She answers with her sexy voice, "Hi, this is Bobbie Jo." I instantly became semi-aroused.

"Hey Bobbie Jo, it's me Bryan from the other night. How are you?" She remembers and is happy I decided to call. We talked for about fifteen minutes and agreed to go out Friday evening. Rick's going to be pissed that I won't be hitting the club with him now. I'm not really sure why, I hardly see the dude once we're there.

Friday night finally arrives. It's been a long week since I first met Bobbie Jo. I'm so stoked to hear her voice and see what she's wearing. It will fun hanging out. Damn, can you hear yourself Bryan? You sound like a pussy whipped bitch. I approach her street and of course, she fucking lives on XXth street. After getting her address and directions, I didn't think this would bother me. A couple minutes go by and I'm still idling at the stop sign trying to turn right. I've taken several deep breathes and I still feel dizzy. The car behind me honks and I'm forced to take my foot off the break, accelerate, and turn right. I keep my head down to avoid that horrifying sign with those pair of wicked snowmen. I did it! I'm not out of the woods yet, because her address is 2XX0 E. XXth street apt X. This has to be some cruel fucking joke. I knew she couldn't be perfect. Walking up to her door wasn't much of a struggle. I just ignored the address above the doorway. The real test came when I arrived at her door. A giant number X staring me down like some nightclub bouncer. I begin to panic and hyperventilate, so I immediately turn around to pull out my phone to text her that I'm at her door. A few minutes go by and she still hasn't answered the door or my text. Still facing the street, I knock to avoid that demonic number. The door opens and I turn around. A thing of beauty has replaced that ugly number. "Hey, my battery died, sorry if you tried to call or text." She explained. She grabs her jacket and shuts the door. Mr. Number X is looking at me like this over-bearing father trying to scare me into returning his daughter untouched. I quickly turn around and walk her to my chick magnet car. She doesn't look that impressed.

Where the hell did this amazing chick come from?

The date was incredible. We didn't stay out too late because she had to go out of town in the morning. We ate a great Italian meal and talked for a couple hours. We people watched while walking around the Grove shopping district. She's got a great sense of humor. On that note, I still believe this is someone's cruel joke because naturally her birthday is August X[th], 19XX. We returned to her apartment and walked up to her door. I don't look at those sinister stacked circles that are trying to prevent me from kissing her. I lean in and her lips are soft and full. What a great night!

The room is full and the circle of freaks are here for a Wednesday night meeting. I guess everyone had a rough weekend. Miguel approaches me and inquires about my date. I told him that the number that comes after seven and before nine surrounds her life. Unbelievable. We take our seats as JoAnn comes into the room. That's when I notice we are short one freak. "Where's Charlie?" I ask with fake concern.

JoAnn quickly replies, "He won't be attending anymore meetings. His new love has elevated him to a place of peace. He's even eaten peanut butter for the first time in years. He liked it. Now who's going to start tonight?"

Before I could speak out, Miguel steals my spotlight. Miguel's fear is a strange one and doesn't affect him often. In fact, he's exposed to it more here talking about it, then on the

outside. His fear is Hippopotomonstrosesquipedaliophobia.
Exactly! Try saying that three times fast. Hell, try saying that one
time slow. What's really twisted is this is the fear of long words.
That means some sadistic prick gave the fear of long words, the
longest word in the history of words. Miguel goes on about
seeing some big word somewhere over the weekend. Finally, he
finishes and it's my turn, but before I could speak, Arctic Brad
blurts out that he's going away with his girlfriend this weekend.
He's excited and scared since it will be in the middle of
mountains. Everyone gives him a congratulatory clap, except for
me. JoAnn gives me a nod to go ahead and begin. I am anxious
for tonight's date; I just want to get through this.

What another great date with Bobbie Jo, but it's
accompanied by a repeat encounter with her creepy chaperone.
We enter her apartment. Ha! Now I'm on the other side of the
door you evil two circled bitch. She goes to the kitchen and I
take a seat on the couch. I need to pause for a moment and
share one of my secrets of hooking up for you amateurs. Every
time you're told to take a seat while she leaves the room to do
something, to get drinks or freshen up, always sit in the middle
of the couch. When she returns she'll have no choice but to sit
right next to you. Trust me. I'm smooth. It never
fails!

Irrational Fears

Bobbie Jo returns with two beers and sits right next to me, works every time. We take a couple sips and sit in uncomfortable silence. Before I could make my move, she pulls me towards her and we begin to passionately kiss. As we continue to get hot and heavy, our clothes find their way to the living room floor. This might be the hardest any Betty has ever made me. She goes down on me and all I can do is stare at her Monet print on the wall. Is it blurry because of this amazing blowjob or is that how it really looks? I'm not really that much into art. She slowly stands up and gives me that I want you look. But then most women do. She turns around and bends over with her perfect ass right in front of me. My focus has gone from art to ass. I stand up, grab her hips, and pull her towards me. That's when my focus went straight back from ass to art. This time it wasn't the blurry landscape thing, it was her ink art. Why did it surprise me that Bobbie Jo, who lives on XXth street, apartment X, born on X-X-XX, has a fucking X-ball tramp stamp? My eyes are stuck on this billiard's ball. I begin to get dizzy and nauseous. The room is spinning and I reach down to grab my shirt from the floor and quickly cover up the new calamitous cockblocker. Crisis averted, X-ball corner pocket.

A beautiful Saturday morning in the city of Angels and I have to sit with the circle of Freaks for over an hour. Well, I should let the group know, that because of this pussy ass fear,

33

I'll probably have to dump this awesome chick. I just can't handle the anxiety of going to her place, the magic X ball above her perfect ass, and even her birthday. I hate that day more than any other. Hell, I'd rather celebrate 911 more than that day. Okay, maybe that's a bit extreme, but I really do hate that fucking day

The meeting is in full swing and the freaks are spewing their silly fears, but I'm not paying attention. Surprisingly the losers are not as annoying as usual. I'll chalk the peace of mind up to the award winning hummer last night. Something seems to be missing. I scan around and the usual freaks are here with some new faces. Wait! Arctic Brad is missing, that's why it's more tolerable. I think he said something about going out of town this weekend. Not ten seconds after that revelation, Armageddon, my name for Meteor John, asks JoAnn about Brad's whereabouts. She informs us that Brad said he won't be returning to our sessions, he's in the mountains... Snow Boarding! Apparently, his girlfriend got him out on the snow. First, Charlie doesn't come back and is eating peanut butter? Now, Arctic Brad is in the mountains snowboarding? "Bryan it's your turn to speak. How's the dating going?" JoAnn asks breaking my concentration. "She's a great girl, but I just can't compete with all those Xs that surround her. I think I have to call it off." I confess to the group.

Irrational Fears

Just after I hear a few moans and groans JoAnn says "Don't give up Bryan; she might help you overcome this fear. Look at Brad and Charlie, they're doing things they never thought they would, because of their girlfriends." I realize that she's absolutely right, it did work for those two clowns, so why not me? I'll give it a shot.

After getting back in town, Bobbie Jo come over to watch The Walking Dead. The show reminds of my fear. The number X gives me the feeling of panic and no escape. Just like the characters in Walking Dead, no escape. I find the show a bit therapeutic. This fear began when I was a child. When I was five, I fell into an abandoned well. It was three days before I was rescued. The number X reminds me of that well every time I see it. Every psychiatrist I've seen says it's because the number X turned sideways is the sign for infinity and its endless looping causes my mind to travel back to that terrible day. If I see an X in passing it's not really a problem. But when my eyes lock onto those double bubbles of trouble, that's when the panic ensues.

We finish watching our show and head straight to the bedroom. I cannot handle that magic X-ball tonight. I'll have to keep her ass out of eyesight. I can't believe I just thought that. Our fuck fest is epic and the repeating cumming clears my head. I realize I need to get over this X-ball situation. We lay there exhausted and weak in the knees. "Bryan, I'm going to my Mother's cabin next weekend, would you like to join me?" Her voice is tempting.

"I'd love to. I could use a break." I answer with boyish excitement.

"I'll pick you up Friday evening." She begins to kiss my neck and rub my cock. Round two.

It was another long week waiting for the get-a-way. Fortunately, the car trip was nice. We talked the whole time so that made it go by fast. She turns onto a small, dark dirt road and drives for about another quarter mile. This is no cabin, it's a huge house. "I can tell it's not what you expected. My Mother has a lot of money and she bought this place many years ago." She explains. We grab our stuff and walk up to a huge and wonderful porch that I'm sure is overlooking some beautiful landscape behind this darkness. The inside is amazing. I already love this place. There is no vile guardian X on the front door. "Make yourself at home and I'll get us a couple of drinks." She says and walks into another room. I take a seat on the massive couch, in the middle of course, and sink into it's incredible cushions. Bobbie Jo returns with two drinks, perfect timing because I'm thirsty. She takes a seat next to me sinking as deep as I did. Oh yes, my favorite, Jack and Coke and it tastes great. She begins to rub my thigh, no wasting time with her. After a few more sips I start to feel extremely tired. I think that long car ride is taking its toll. Damn, I can't keep my eyes open and I can't feel her hand rubbing my thigh anymore. I feel strange. Oh, shit! I think she slipped me a mickey. I've been Bill Cosbyed.

My vision is coming back to me but everything's still a blur, like that Monet print. I can't move my arms or legs. Two female voices are talking but I can't make out what they're saying. I manage to turn my head to the left and discover that I'm being wheeled down a hallway in a wheelchair. I can finally make out what one of the voices is saying, "He's starting to wake up, let's get him into room 8." Room X? That's not good at all. We pass a window and I see Charlie from the group. What is he doing here? He's sitting still with his head down on a table in the middle of the room surrounded by several jars of peanut butter. Are these bitches making him eat peanut butter? They keep pushing me down the hall, I can't see their faces, but by the sound of the angelic voice, I know one is Bobbie Jo. I struggle to move my head to the right to get a glimpse of another window. The room is full of snow and looks really cold. Suddenly Arctic Brad appears and bangs on the glass. He doesn't see me. These aren't windows, these are one-way mirrors. We are prisoners. Arctic Brad looks like he's freezing

and for the first time I actually feel bad for him. I want to help
him, but I can't, I have my own issues with room number X.

They leave me sitting here in my wheelchair. Room X is
poorly lit and chilly. I'm starting to regain function in my arms
and legs. I need to give myself a few more minutes before
standing. Suddenly the lights come on. I see the walls, covered
with thousands of that bastard number. I instantly start looking
down at the ground only to see the dreadful number covering
the floor. My next option is to close my eyes. It works until I
hear Bobbie Jo's voice. Even though she's probably brought me
to my death, her voice still turns me on. Bitch! "Bryan, as you
can see by now you're surrounded by your worst fear. In order
to escape this room you must overcome it. Behind one of those
number Xs lies your salvation, your relief, and your freedom."
This is confusing, how the fuck does she know about my
problem? I only shared my man-meat with her. Then I hear the
second woman's voice, it's familiar.

Holy shit! It's JoAnn, "Bryan, I know you can do this.
This is my new radical treatment to rid people of their fears. You
might hate me now but when you're free you'll thank me. I
believe that facing your fear or to die by not trying is the best
treatment one can have. Look around, you're not in that well
anymore." She's absolutely right, I do hate her. I begin to crawl
and feel every number X in sight, physically and mentally. The

room is spinning and I want to puke my guts out. Then something dawns on me. Something that's more disturbing than this room. I laugh hysterically. The 8's no longer matter, the puking stops and I dry heave between laughs. Bobbie Jo is also the same chick that brought Brad and Charlie here. That means she banged them too. I got their sloppy seconds! Fucking Dino!

To Swallow a Fly

By Katherine Hannula Hill

The police want to know why I brought a horse into my house. Alfred is the largest and the prettiest of my horses. His coat the color of dried blood. The two policemen face me and I smile at them, stretching my smirk into a mask of silence and mystery. I'll never tell. They'll never find it. At first, they think they can break me: *How long has your husband been gone? Where did he go? Why is his truck parked in front of the barn?* The best thing to do is give the cops nothing to go on, nothing but a wide smile. I sit back in my uncomfortable chair, surveying the barren interrogation room. I'm pleased it's going so well. I've never tested my smile's strength for this long, but it's holding up quite nicely. The cops begin to grow impatient, leaving the room to give me time to "think it over." I'm no fool. I watch TV. I know they're still watching when they're not there, so I just keep smiling, even when it's just the mirror and me.

I'm sure it slipped in the door when the cop left, but I didn't notice it until now. I'm one of the few people whose ears move like an animal. Since I was a child, if I hear an unfamiliar noise my ears would go back, and if I were listening intently, my head would tilt to the side and wait. That's how it was every night. I'd lie in bed, tilting my head for the sound of the truck door slamming and waiting for the front door to open. Without seeing him, I could see the lipstick on his collar and smell the beer on his breath. I could feel my ears press back as he began to hum.

It stays silent for a minute, quiet and thinking I won't notice it. Then it moves. My ears perk and my head tilts. They know. My smile decompresses and I glare at the mirror. How could they know? I was so careful... The smile tugs at my lips again as I remember the fools I'm dealing with but it quickly disappears. It moved again. They know. They've sent it here to torment me, to make me talk. It pauses and lies silent again. I scan the room trying to connect the sound to its source. When my eyes don't help, I shut them, listening. The noise. It moves close beside me. And then I see it, its tiny, black body moving towards me from the wall, bouncing clumsily against the light before landing next to me on the table. I try to smile again but the buzzing won't let me. How can I smile when I know they know when they're watching me behind that mirror, waiting for the noise to get to me, to make me confess. The knife. The barn. And worst of all, the humming of the fly.

I was so careful. I did everything right. They can't know. I begin to relax, remembering how cunning I'd been, how I'd planned it all out, lured him there, squeezed him in the box, sealed it up, spread the cloth over it and smiled. But the clunk of fly against light, the buzz of its disgusting body reminds me of my one flaw. A fly escaped. Just as I was sealing up the box—the knife and my husband inside—it flew out. All evidence was supposed to be safely locked inside that box, which I planned to drag to the truck and drive to our apple orchards. Our acres and acres of apple orchards where I would bury him where no one would think to look—beside his favorite tree. Sure, people would've asked me where he was, but how many times can people politely ask the wife of a cheating drunk where he'd run off to this time? The poor dear didn't know. Poor thing had been completely deserted on a big farm by her no-good husband. She'd be pitied, not suspected. It was the perfect plan. Until that fly flew out. They'd find it—wherever it went. His DNA on its' disgusting little legs, maybe some of his blood in its disgusting little body. Eventually it would be smashed and they'd bring in a blood spatter analyst and a DNA test and suddenly the poor deserted housewife would be a suspect. Put on trial. Sentenced. No, I had to make sure I trapped that fly and kept the evidence away from anyone who could use it against me. It wasn't the drinking or the cheating. It wasn't the late nights. I was happiest on my own, at peace with the sound of the lake and the view of our apple trees. It was what he did when he got home.

Irrational Fears

It started the night he came home singing that song, "Barbara Ann." Missing every high note and yelling—not singing— the "bop bop bop"s. One nightly entrance would've been bad enough, but it went on for days. After a week, it diminished to a hum, a constant, repetitive hum. The sound lasted for a month. It forced my ears back and my mouth to curl up in a snarl until I finally fell asleep. Even then, it would haunt my dreams: 'Ba, ba, ba, ba, Barbara Ann...' I knew this wouldn't do. And that's when I caught myself thinking in the lyrics of the song. A part of me believed things couldn't get more unbearable until the song stopped and something tuneless took its place. A sound in the throat moving up and down, down and up, never repeating, never nearing a melody, just unceasing sound. Please understand, before this, at peace with the lapping lake and acres of apples and horses to care for, I would never have even dreamt of hurting a fly.

But no one could live with that misery. I made the plan. I built the box. I hid the knife. I broke a hole in the roof of the barn and woke him from his hungover sleep, dragging him to the barn with the excuse of fixing it before it rained. All had gone just as I'd planned till that fly and its disgusting body escaped. I knew I couldn't just squish the thing, leaving its evidence on the wall or under my shoe. I needed to dispose of it in just the right way. And that's when I noticed the spider, perched in its web, under the light. I knew if I could just coax the fly into the web, the spider would devour it. Not even the cleverest cop would think to look in the belly of a spider. I was smart enough to know the worst thing I could do was open the barn door and let it escape. No, it was best to just sit and wait. Wait for that fly to do just what the one in this interrogation room is doing: fly towards the light. Entice and fool it with that light, sending it straight into the spider's clutches. For what may have been an hour I sat still beneath the light, shooing the fly back in its direction whenever it came near me. With a clang, the buzzing stopped, and the fly fell, finally trapped in the web. I'm not sure who was more pleased with this development, me or the spider that scurried over.

When the spider finished its feast, no doubt licking all eight of its long legs in satisfaction, it headed back to its corner. I was there waiting for it with an old mason jar. Scooping it up quickly, I let it drop to the bottom of the jar, before twisting the lid tightly. I placed it in the passenger seat to accompany me on my ride to the open grave awaiting my husband.

As I pulled back into the driveway, I began to check off my to-do list: Body-hidden. Murder weapon-buried by my favorite tree a mile away from his. Traces of blood-burned along with the tarp placed on the barn floor.

Irrational Fears

I sat at the kitchen table, the creature in the glass jar my last obstacle. The spider was the only piece of evidence that remained. From the hallway, I could hear the ghost of Barbara Ann, still audible in the succession of irritating tweets coming from a large metal cage. I smiled, thinking I could kill two birds-- so to speak-- with one stone. I walked to the cage, where the parakeet was whistling away, bobbing its head to the rhythm. I carefully removed the lid from the jar before placing it, and the unsuspecting spider, inside the cage. The spider, thrilled by its sudden freedom, quickly crawled out. The parakeet let out another tweet of satisfaction.

Even with the spider gone, my mastermind was not yet satisfied. It demanded not a trace of evidence and nothing less would be acceptable. So I left the parakeet's cage open in the closet—with our cat.

The cat, who had been kicked out of the warm house long ago, was so happy to be let back in. When I let it out of the closet, it curled up contentedly beside the fire and purred. I stared at it, unsatisfied. I needed that cat gone. Not dead. Just not here, for the cops to find and scan. I wanted her curled up and content somewhere else. So I let in the old sheepdog, but the cat didn't seem to mind and simply jumped up to where she was sure to be out of its reach. So I brought in the goat to stomp around. That startled the poor thing, but she still felt safe enough to simply put her back to it and snooze with one eye open. I needed bigger and louder. The cow was the final straw, but instead of sending the cat outside, it sent the thing into a frenzy. Soon I had hissing cat, yelping dog, stomping goat, and mooing cow colliding into each other and breaking everything in the living room. That's when I brought in Alfred, whose massive weight and giant hooves would soon make some peace out of the chaos I'd created. Soon the cat, chased by dog, were out of the house. A threatening kick from Alfred and the goat was on its way. The cow didn't need much prodding, and walked out of the front door. I gave Alfred some grateful pats, and sat down on the couch, surveying the damage with a happy smile. That would keep the cat from ever coming back. She'd be driven away to the neighbors, where that sweet, empty-headed heifer next door would take her in as she did all the stray cats that came whining for fresh milk. There she'd remain completely unconnected and unsuspected, and the one piece of evidence would spend years purring and sipping milk before it met its end. Finally buried along with the rest of the crime. I had just put the bridle on Alfred and begun to lead him back outside when the police arrived. Apparently, I'd created quite a disturbance.

It must have been the barmaid, whose best tipping customer hadn't been in for three nights, who called in to report a missing person. The cat hadn't been back in all that time. The police left that first day, content they'd done their duty, after I let them know that all the commotion was just a couple animals in the house—nothing to worry about. But they came back. I smiled at them when they took me in for questioning just as I'm smiling again now, remembering that cat. Whatever they think they know, a silly little fly won't get anything out of me. I'll never tell.

The fly has landed on the mirror, and looks eerily like a bullet in the middle of my forehead, but I simply stare through my reflection and smile wider. I'll never tell.

Blind Man's Bluff

By Paul Rhodes

*H*azel takes me by the wrist, leading my hand slowly to the freshly boiled kettle. She guides my fingers to the handle and the two of us pour hot water into the mugs on the table.

"Thanks for helping, Eddie," she says, replacing the kettle. "You stir the two coffees, they're right in front of you, and I'll put milk in the teas."

Running my fingers along the counter tops I find the kitchen door and hold it open as Hazel passes through, carrying the tray of hot drinks.

"You're such a gentleman," she smiles, "what would I do without you?"

Noticing me struggling without my white stick, Hazel sets the tray down and returns, guiding me back to my desk. "Are you coming for drinks on Friday?" she asks. "We love having you along with us."

I tell her sure, I'll come for a beer, put my headphones on and hit RETURN on my keyboard.

Irrational Fears

"YOU HAVE ONE UNREAD EMAIL!" the robotic voice screams at me as my body recoils, forcing the mouthful of hot tea into the back of my nose.

"LEFT CLICK TO READ NOW, RIGHT CLICK TO SAVE FOR LATER!" it blasts, like Stephen Hawking doing crowd control through a bullhorn.

I wipe the tea dripping from my nostrils and reposition my sunglasses. Jimmy the office clown sniggers in his chair behind me.

"Sorry, Ed," he laughs, leaning back to pat me on the shoulder. "You left your system unlocked and I couldn't resist... it's me, Jimmy, by the way - you know that, right?"

I've been blind for months now. At work anyway...

"You're such an asshole, Jimmy," Hazel says, as she hurries to my desk and places a small wad of tissues in my hand. I look past her and smile a puppy-dog-that-has-just-shit-on-the-rug kind of smile.

She gives my arm a gentle squeeze and glides back to her desk, her ass swaying from side to side beneath the grey woolen pencil skirt that stops just above her knee.

All the guys in the office want to fuck Hazel.

They glare hungrily as she leans over my desk in her tight knitted vest tops, exposing a glimpse of her white bra and smooth tan skin. She laughs at my silly jokes as I bring my lunch

49

from the fridge. She lets me run my fingers over the features of her face. Down the bridge of her nose, along her jaw-line, through that thick curly brown hair. Sometimes her intense beauty is too much, I get out of and sorts and rattle across the office floor, thrashing my white stick against the wall as I go, out to the disabled toilet where I sit and jerk off, the scent of her still on my hands.

I had no idea that blind guys got so much attention from hot girls. It has become a childlike openness usually reserved for their fathers and gay men.

Speaking of fathers, I should thank my own.

My Dad was a nut for Greek mythology. While other kids were tucked up in bed listening to softly spoken renditions of Jack and the Beanstalk or Cinderella, my Dad was traumatizing me with visceral interpretations of Pandora's Box, the Minotaur, and his personal favorite, Medusa. My younger brother Marcus would fall asleep soon after the stories began, but I was gripped. Watching my Dad creep around in the shadows, holding the lamp to his face. His fingers mimicking snakes for hair, the cold dead stare of Medusa peering into the lower bunk where I lie.

It was around that time that my sleep paralysis started. I'd wake up terrified, locked in some awful nightmare with

Medusa towering over me being trapped inside my body, unable to move – turned to stone.

"His mind is just a little active," the doctor told my parents. "He'll grow out of it."

But I didn't, and I knew his diagnosis was wrong. There were Gorgons everywhere, and there was no way I was going to spend my life as a human statue.

My parents thought I was crazy so it was down to me to protect myself; eventually I stopped making eye contact with people.

And when the night terrors came, I would repeat the mantra *I am Perseus*, and imagine holding up Medusa's severed head by her dead snake hair before those that doubted me.

Faking blindness? That came later.

Leaving the office that evening, Hazel stops me in the foyer.

"Can I give you a ride home, Eddie?" she asks. "Or if you need to go to the supermarket, I could take you there?"

She smiles awkwardly, and through the lenses of my sunglasses, I can see her cheeks reddening.

What is it with this girl, is she trying to bank karma points?

I tell Hazel no thanks; I'm going to go meet someone. She looks disappointed and insists on punching my address into her phone, telling me that she'll be outside my building in her car at 8:30 tomorrow morning.

I say goodbye and walk away, tapping my white stick on the pavement. In front of me is my car, parked several streets away. Hazel drives past and sounds her horn, as a sightless might, I wave in the opposite direction.

***

I started pretending to be blind after a run of unsuccessful job interviews. Prospective employers look for a couple things with potential employees – a firm handshake and eye contact. Unfortunately, my affliction prevented me from delivering one of them.

I only had to be in the room for a few minutes to know that the interviewer had written me off. Mostly they'd speed up, rattling through their questions as quickly as possible, not writing my answers down, and sometimes not even waiting until I'd finished speaking before moving on.

The constant rejection was getting me down, the same feedback over and over.

You have the skills and experience that we are looking for; it's just that you appeared to lack confidence at the interview.

A couple of times I tried to explain I didn't want to risk being turned to stone by making eye contact with a Gorgon disguised as a human being. But that just made things worse.

Occasionally, an employer would see my unwillingness to engage as some kind of fucked up challenge and play a bizarre cat and mouse game of trying to force eye contact with me – ducking down, bobbing from side to side like a boxer, standing in place, shaking their hand, and looking anywhere but at them.

One guy just couldn't let it go and I ran out of the interview, covering my eyes with my hands, yelling for him to stop.

Then one fateful day while flicking through the Kent Messenger I found a job ad for government analysts.

One particular paragraph caught my attention:

We are committed to the employment and career development of disabled people. If you tell us that you are disabled, we can make reasonable adjustments at each stage of the recruitment and selection process and, if you join us, to where and how you work.

I read the advert over and over.

If you tell us that, you are disabled.

Irrational Fears

I discovered that the British government has a Guaranteed Interview Scheme for anyone that claims to have a disability.

Thanks to the Equalities Act 2010, they can no longer ask to see your medical records before offering you a job.

Sitting there in that government interview, eyes hidden behind sunglasses, white stick lying on the floor next to me, I knew the job was mine.

The kind words on how impressive my qualifications were – given my circumstances. I enjoyed the sympathetic sigh from across the table when I told the HR lady how getting this job would be a dream come true. Something I would never have imagined possible. Wiping away imaginary tears from behind my sunglasses I remember wondering – can blind people cry?

***

"Mind your backs ladies and gents," Howard says, carefully setting the tray of beers down on the table.

Hazel leans over and picks up one of the pints. Howard, still standing, flashes a quick glimpse at her tits squeezed inside a tight glittery vest top. She places the beer in front of me, gently wrapping my hand around the cold glass.

"There you go, Eddie, happy Friday everyone!" she says, raising her own glass.

It's pretty decent being the only blind guy in the group. When it's my turn to buy a round I hand the money to Howard or Steve and they go to the bar for me.

Sometimes they get my round in and refuse to take any money at all.

"It's cool, Ed," they say, "we're just glad you came along, it can't be easy..."

Hazel recently broke up with her boyfriend. She didn't seem too bothered by it though.

"I think I'm done with the pumped-up macho types," she says, laughing at the exaggerated grins and high fives of the public servant nerds seated around our table.

"The next guy I date is going to be different – thoughtful and kind, with a good sense of humour." She winks at me, and I wonder if I've been rumbled until she quickly looks away embarrassed, realising her mistake.

The beers flow and I begin working my way through my repertoire of blind jokes.

The first guy to convince a blind man he needed sunglasses must have been one hell of a salesman!

It's amazing what people will laugh at when you are mocking your own disability.

Why don't blind people skydive? It scares the hell out of the dog.

Watching from across the table as Hazel and the others laugh and tell me how hysterical I am, Jimmy decides he wants in on the action too.

"If blind people wear dark glasses, why don't deaf people wear earmuffs?" he offers, looking around the table for approval.

Silence.

"C'mon Jimmy, that's a bit off," frowns Miles, as the others shake their heads and mutter disapprovingly.

Hazel rubs my back sympathetically, like she's just told me my grandmother has died.

I let Jimmy squirm for a bit, his face full of blood. Then I grin at him from across the table.

"Jesus Jimmy, I didn't see that one coming!"

And everyone falls about laughing again as Jimmy takes a long pull on his beer, peeking over the rim of the pint glass, making sure all is forgiven.

***

Staggering out into the still winter night with Hazel, arm in arm like contestants in a three legged race, I give up using my white stick.

She's drunk now and doesn't notice me leading the way without guidance.

We share a taxi back to my place and she woozily accepts my offer to come inside.

We make out on my bed for a little bit, her mouth sloppy and wet, and when I get back from taking a piss I find her passed out beneath the duvet. I peel one of her eyelids back to see what shade of blue her eyes are.

***

The next morning, Hazel presses down on my chest and digs her knees in tight just below my ribs. My kidneys feel ready to burst and I let out an involuntary whimper.

"No, no, no...not yet," she gasps, "I just need a few more minutes."

Sex with Hazel should come with a health warning.

Mistaking my yelp for ecstatic rapture and sensing the ride is coming to an end, Hazel speeds up. Her fingers digging deep behind my collarbone. Her hips grinding forward and back. Her hands reaching around my throat as I pray for her to choke me unconscious.

Wedged in the death-grip of her thighs, it's clear why she's chosen me. She's sick of tough guy boyfriends pushing her about; she wants to be in charge for once. She found what she needed – a total pussy that will always depend on her for everything.

Hazel pushes her forehead against mine, our noses crushed together. Slowly her eyelids begin to open...and I freak the fuck out, throwing her off me and leaping out of bed - standing there naked, shaking out my arms and legs, making sure they're not turning to stone.

"Eddie? Are you OK?' Hazel asks, watching me, with a strange, startled expression.

"Yeah, just cramp," I say, remembering that I'm blind. I feel my way back to her like some kind of feral mime, flipping her onto her belly, clutching her hips...

I grab a handful of her hair but it turns into snakes, furious to be woken, hissing and lunging, fangs dripping with venom. And I close my eyes telling myself:

I am Perseus. I am Perseus. I am Perseus.

Hazel moans as I get my rhythm back, hard and fast, trying to finish. Her body stutters and arches and she slides face first into the pillow.

I flop down next to her and we lie there together, her face buried in my neck.

I need a plan if I'm going to sustain this.

Perhaps in a couple months I'll take a few weeks off work, maybe visit some radical Eastern European doctor who's pioneering a new form of corrective eye surgery. I'll return to work with bandages covering my eyes. And slowly, I'll get my

vision back. Hazel, I'll say, you're more beautiful than I could
ever have dreamed.

Then I'll only have my Medusa complex to deal with.

"You have the prettiest green eyes," Hazel breathes.
"I've never seen them before, they're always hidden behind
your Ray-bans. Will you leave them off for a while?"

***

A bit later, I'm slowly working my way around the
kitchen, making breakfast. I spill tea and drop an egg on the
floor, trying not to make it look too easy.

"Are you sure I can't help?" Hazel asks, sitting at the
living room table, wearing only my faded Afghan Whigs t-shirt
and her white lace panties.

She closes her eyes and takes a deep, exaggerated
breath as I set the plate of bacon and scrambled eggs in front of
her. "That smells incredible," she says, "you know, watching you
cook like that...you're a real inspiration, Eddie."

I keep my eyes trained on her fork while she's eating.

As it's just about to reach her lips, I look at her eyes.
Nearly everyone looks down a split second before they put a
forkful of food into their mouth. Just to make sure that the food
isn't going to slide off and ruin a fancy outfit or dribble down
their chin like they're some uncivilised retard.

I look at Hazel's eyes for that split second, and then glance down at my fork as she looks back up again.

We're like two wooden figures on a cuckoo clock, facing each other, bowing in turn.

Why couldn't I have met you at school, Hazel? When the other kids were poking fun at me, calling me names? And when the teachers would shout, *"look me in the eye when I'm talking to you, Edward!"*

You would have made it right, Hazel. I know you would.

***

That evening, driving along the A2 towards Canterbury to meet my brother, my mind is full of Hazel.

Throughout my life, my Medusa complex has alienated me from girls. Before Hazel, the few that I attracted were deranged, frightening people with a proclivity for self-destruction.

One of them, Kimberley, snuck rat poison into our Cokes while we were at the movies so we could spend eternal damnation together. Fortunately, she got the dose wrong and we spent the night puking charcoal in the emergency room.

Kimberley went to jail. There was no second date.

The most recent was Becky, a germaphobe. She pulled the emergency brake lever on a train we were riding because a guy a few seats away sneezed without covering his mouth. The jolt threw me from my seat on to the lady sat opposite, breaking her nose.

Becky was sectioned and I was alone again.

Walking into the busy pub, I feel self-conscious without my sunglasses. I see Marcus waiting for me at the pool table. He's already set the balls up and two full pints of beer are waiting for us at a small table. Marcus and I have never talked about my inability to make eye contact; he's always just accepted me for who I am.

Scanning the pub for Gorgons I notice a blind lady sat at the bar talking to a friend, her golden retriever guide dog lying curled at her feet, wearing a yellow fluorescent harness. Glaring at me intently - *You fake ass prick,* the dog seems to say, *you think it's all a game, don't you?*

chalk my cue and pot two easy red balls left over the centre pockets after Marcus' break. Shot after shot, the red balls keep dropping. I finish with a perfect long shot on the black, blasting it straight up the table and into the top right corner pocket with a satisfying crack.

"Ed, check out that girl in the corner, I think she's impressed," says Marcus, gesturing somewhere behind me. "She hasn't taken her eyes off you the whole time, she's hot too."

Standing there, casually chalking the tip of my cue, I glance over.

Marcus is right. She is looking our way. But not in a *Hi there, want to buy me a drink?* Kind of way. Hers is a look of horror, mouth open wide. Her friend, a plump, freckly, redhead, is nudging her, asking, *are you OK?*

Some luck.

Pretending I haven't seen her I turn back towards Marcus, ready to suggest moving on to another pub, but he's already racking the balls up for our next game.

"Challenger breaks," he says, lining up the cue and the white ball.

The dog, smirking now, slides on to his belly, getting comfortable for the big show. The look in his eyes says it all — *you fucked up, son.*

I feel a light tap on my shoulder — Hazel. She looks possessed, jaw dropped, face frozen in time by trauma.

"You said last night you'd be here…" she mumbles, "when you were drunk…I thought I'd surprise…" she trails off into a whisper.

"Hazel? Is that you?" I ask, looking all around like I'm in total darkness. I raise my hands to her face.

Hazel loses it.

"Bastard!" she screams, slapping me hard across the face, grabbing hold of my shirt. Desperate to avoid eye contact with her, I start thrashing about trying to break free, but it's no good.

"Hey, what's going on?" yells Marcus from across the pool table.

But Hazel's too far gone to hear him.

"You're blind!" she yells, shaking me back and forth, "you're fucking blind...how could you do this, you've lied to everyone!"

Her big red friend is here now, glaring at me furiously, rubbing Hazel's back, telling her to come sit down. She attempts to pries her fingers from my shirt, but Hazel isn't letting go.

"I defended you, you asshole! Jimmy said he saw you looking at your watch but I told him he was drunk...why have you even got a watch, anyway?"

Sobbing now, and with the attention of the whole pub, Hazel slowly lets go of my shirt, her fury fading into dismay and sadness and the indignation you feel as a child when someone tells you that Santa's not real and it shatters your whole world.

"It's a special watch," I stammer, "it talks to me and..."

The second slap lands harder than the first and I taste blood in my mouth. This is the final straw for Big Red who grabs hold of Hazel and drags her towards the pub door writhing and shrieking, flailing her arms about like she's on fire.

"What the fuck was that about?" Asks Marcus, as the screams of *bastard* become nothing more than a forlorn howl from the car park.

"I've never seen her before in my life," I tell him, "Let's get out of here…"

"But the game, I'm winning…"

"Fuck the game, I surrender, come on, I'll give you a ride home."

Driving out the car park, we see Hazel and Big Red across the street, huddled together. Hazel looks like she's struggling to breathe.

She spots us, her eyes bulge wildly as she starts screaming and cursing again.

"He's got a car! He can fucking drive! I've been going five miles out of my way twice a fucking day to get him to and from work!"

From the rearview mirror, I watch as her body crumples to the floor.

Leaving Hazel wailing on the curb, Big Red throws her shoes off and chases our car down the street, yelling obscenities.

***

It's late by the time I get home. Sitting on my couch alone in the dark, my stomach knots and I dry heave uncontrollably.

Not for Hazel, not really.

I'm going to miss being blind. In many ways it's freed me.

People treat me so much better now that I wear sunglasses indoors and fumble around with my white stick. They're kind to me, more patient. They bring me little trinkets back from their holidays.

I saw this and thought of you, here hold it; can you tell what it is?

Even Jimmy, the office asshole, gives me less shit than he gives everyone else. Jimmy Watson, the guy that wolf-whistles whenever Miles the gay guy from accounts walks into the room. Yeah, he occasionally screws with the volume of my computer, but he also asks if I want anything from the shop on his way out at lunchtime. He lets me know when my shoes come untied.

Hazel will tell everyone about my ruse and I'll lose my job. And then I'm right back where I started—the weirdo that avoids people. A guy who never really builds a relationship with anyone because he's scared they are going to turn him to stone.

Sorry Hazel, I don't think I can see you again.

I dial 999, ask the operator to send an ambulance, and give my address. When the lady asks what the emergency is I hang up.

Try moving a knife blade close enough to your face for the tip to touch your eyeball. Your brain's inbuilt defense mechanism that's designed to save you from yourself won't allow it.

A spoon however, gets the brain all confused.

What kind of damage can he do to me with a spoon, the inner machinations wonder.

And really it doesn't hurt, not that much. It's uncomfortable for sure. Although the sound is unbearable, the dull twang of those sinewy bits that hold the eyeball in its socket, stretching and snapping as I dig deeper and deeper.

After scooping out as much as I can from my ocular cavities I sit at the table where I served Hazel bacon and eggs this morning, and wait for the paramedics to arrive. My cheeks are wet and blood is dripping on to my hands.

I have never known darkness like this. It's beautiful - peaceful, transcendent and all the panic and sadness is gone.

Everything I do now, from catching the bus to baking a cake will be a major fucking achievement. I will forever be a hero to somebody.

And no one will ever be able to turn me to stone.

Why didn't I think of this sooner?

I'll take Monday off, maybe Tuesday too. Hazel can have those days. She can run around the office telling everyone about what I've been up to, and how I've deceived them all. And they can hug her, fawn over her, stare at her tits, and tell each other that I'm disgusting, that they knew it all along.

On Wednesday, I'll use my trusty white stick to guide me to my desk as everyone in the office watches in silence. I'll switch on my computer, take off my sunglasses for the very first time at work, turn to them all with a nice big shit-eating grin and ask...

Who wants tea?

The Hand of John

By Matthew Lett

Morris Flynn had a problem. It wasn't a serious problem, at least not yet, but it was still weighing on his mind like a millstone. It didn't involve money (as so many problems arise from) or his 2-year relationship with his current girlfriend or even his career at the Leviathan Printing Corp. where Morris worked as a graphics design artist.

It was none of these. Where the problem lies---or *floated* to be more exact---was in the toilet of his office building. The building itself was two stories tall and erected in the late 1800's; a smaller structure than most when considering the high-rises built around it. The solitary bathroom with its twin toilets was located on the second floor, and it was here where Morris's troubles began.

It had been over a week since he'd first made his discovery and even now he could scarcely believe it without thinking that he might need serious psychiatric counseling. Morris had seen (and was still seeing) a hand inside the toilet bowl of stall number two. Stall number one had been blocked off for weeks due to repairs, and with his irritable bowel syndrome kicking up its heels; Morris had found himself with no other option but to address the situation.

But how? How does a person rationalize the sudden appearance of a hand inside a toilet bowl when apparently no one else had seen it, or if they had, even bothered to mention it? How indeed?

Morris was standing outside of stall number two now, his hands placed firmly on his hips, his brow scrunched into furrows of concentration. He could see just over the lip of the toilet and knew that if he took a step closer he'd get the full picture. The hand would still be there, floating in its make-shift aquarium like some obscene aquatic wildlife. But he didn't need to see it. He could hear it splashing in the bowl like a child taking a bath, an awful, eerie sound that echoed though the bathroom.

...*splish! splash! splish! splash!*...

And what didn't make sense (as if any of this made sense to Morris's rational mind) was that the hand hadn't been dismembered. It was attached to an arm; a muscular arm with long ropey muscles like cables that disappeared below the wrist. But Morris didn't need to see the entire arm. He knew the hand was attached to something---*or someone*---and had no desire to find out what that something might be.

Irrational Fears

Suppose the hand belonged to an informant for the FBI who'd been whacked by the Mob? What then? What if they'd just cut the poor guy's arm off and thrown it in the sewer? Was it even possible for an arm/hand to travel that far and then up the drainage pipe of an office toilet?

Morris thought about it, still peeking over the lip of the toilet...

...*splish! splash! splish! splash!*...

...and after careful consideration decided the idea was ludicrous. But how could it not be true? The damn thing was in there splashing around like a trout on a hook! And to add insult to injury (if that were possible given the situation) the index finger on the hand was wearing a signet ring. The ring was gold in color and had the symbol of a pyramid in its center.

Despite his intentions, Morris took a step closer.

The hand was still there, of course. It was floating there on top of the water with its withered fingers and long, curved fingernails that resembled the talons of a vulture. A finger (the one with the golden ring, no less) rose up and seemed to identify Morris. It pointed at him as if to say, "*There you are!*" and then waggled itself back and forth like an upset mother scolding her child found in the proverbial cookie jar.

Morris thought about trying to flush it, to get rid of it in any way possible. The idea terrified him, afraid that if he tried

70

that the hand would reach up and lock itself about his wrist. And then what? What if he did manage to flush it while struggling with the hand but it wouldn't go down? Would he scream and break free, or would the hand drag him down the drain into a dark, watery grave teeming with rats and cockroaches?

That was too many questions with too few answers, and Morris wasn't itching to try anything. But there was another problem. One of a more immediate nature. He had to crap--- plain and simple. His guts were in knots, cramping and pleading to be let loose, and if it didn't happen soon, those same guts would rebel in a flush of something that he didn't want to think about.

The hand splashed again, almost playfully as if enjoying itself, when the door to the men's room opened. The hand froze, and so did Morris. He watched as it made a slow turn like the eye of a periscope, sensing its surroundings. And then with a twitter of its long fingers, the hand disappeared with a soft *plip*! Back down into its murky domain.

Morris stood there staring at the toilet in fascination, unaware that he was being talked to. He knew what he'd just seen was impossible---if not to mention insane---but he also knew on a more primitive level, somewhere deep in the folds of

his psyche when men were still evolving from the apes, that
what had just happened might be...plausible?

"Morris? You okay? You look a bit pale, man."

Morris turned his face slack and blank. He looked like
a man waking from a nightmare. He could see James Blakely
from accounting standing there, watching him with either
suspicion or concern. Maybe both.

"You okay?" James repeated. "Looks like you've seen
a ghost."

Nodding his head, Morris forced a smile. His gut hurt,
and on top of it, he really didn't like Blakely that much. Blakely
was a snitch. A busybody around the office with nothing better
to do than to run around spreading gossip. To tell Blakely
something---*anything*---was akin to writing an inter-office e-mail
to the other associates explaining your masturbation problem.
In other words, he would have to be careful.

"Yeah, James," Morris agreed, "something like that.
Just having a little stomach trouble, you know?"

Blakely was nodding his head as if he understood
perfectly. "I know what you mean, man," he said. "I had a touch
of the flu a few months ago, and when I tell you it was coming
out both ends, I mean it!" He snorted laughter while unzipping
his fly. "I just came in to drain the tamale."

That's lizard, dimwit, Morris thought, but said nothing. He stepped aside as Blakely brushed past him and entered stall number two. He wondered briefly if the hand would make a special guest appearance; if it would pop out of the toilet bowl with a cheery "*Hi-Ho!*" and point at Blakely in its accusing manner. Morris doubted it, but it sure as hell would have given Blakely something to talk about!

"Did you hear about that new administrative assistant that works for Carlson?" Blakely's voice echoed. Morris could hear the man's urine hitting the toilet and was also hoping that he'd hear a startled scream from the stall. But no such luck. Blakely went on talking. "You know the pretty little thing that he hired last week?"

"I haven't met her yet," Morris answered, "But I did see her. She seems pleasant enough."

Blakely laughed. "Guess what?"

Morris cringed as another cramp hit him, thinking people like Blakely always started off juicy tidbits of gossip with "*Guess what?*"

"I hear she's into leather."

"Leather?" Morris asked. The last time he'd seen the young lady she'd been dressed in a pretty yellow skirt with a white blouse, but no leather.

The stream of Blakely's urine tapered off, and then stopped with a tiny dripping sound. "Yeah, leather," Blakely said. "You know: underwear, whips, hoods, stuff like that? Something you always wanted your woman to wear but were too afraid to ask." He laughed again as if he'd told a particularly funny joke. Morris failed to see the humor.

Blakely went on incessantly as he almost always did. "I also heard she's a freak. Know what I mean? She likes her men rough and her sex even rougher. In fact, if you ask me" (which was another common nomenclature for the true gossiper) "I'd say Carlson hired her for..."

Morris went for broke. He was tired of listening to Blakely's fantasies and assumptions, and with Blakely being a self-proclaimed authority on most subjects (not to mention the object of scorn in his peer's eyes), Morris thought the man might be a source of information.

"James," he said, "you ever see anything...well...weird in here?"

There was a pause, then the sound of the toilet flushing. Morris could just imagine the hand at the bottom of the bowl swirling round and round like a ship caught in a whirlpool. *Maybe it'll drown*, he thought, but knew that was wishful thinking.

"Weird? Blakely asked. He stepped out, zipping up his fly. A small wet spot stained his crotch. "Like what?"

Morris shrugged, uncertain of how to proceed. Anything he told James Blakely would be taken literally, be it fact or fiction, and if he wasn't careful he'd find himself sitting in Carlson's office answering some difficult questions. Robert Carlson was the office manager at the Leviathan Printing Corp, a rough and tough guy who wore his hair in a year-round burr and was known to be somewhat of a prude. He was also an ex-Marine officer with a no bullshit rule. When it came to asking questions and getting to the bottom of things Carlson was the consummate professional. Morris didn't need that action.

"It's hard to explain," Morris said. "But I think something's going on around here."

"Where?" Blakely asked. "Here in the building?"

"Not exactly." Morris felt as if he were walking in a minefield at midnight, where the footing was treacherous and a false step could get you blown to smithereens. "Like I said, it's hard to explain."

"What's hard to explain? Did you hear something? Are people talking?"

Morris could see the hard gleam of greed in the man's eyes; a shiny, waxy look that reflected Blakely's need and desire for carnal knowledge. "No, nobody's talking about anything," Morris replied, "but I think—"

"Well, I've heard things, buddy," Blakely interjected. He was good at interruptions except when talking with Carlson. Carlson would've slapped him. "Some mighty strange things let me tell you! For instance, do you know when this building was built?"

Morris shook his head, still thinking about the hand with its gold ring and curved fingernails and what it might be up to. Could it be listening? Was it even there? Really?

"It was built in eighteen eighty-five," Blakely said, "and do you know what it was built on?"

Morris stared at him. He had no idea what the man was talking about. The building itself was located on the block of 4th and Detroit Avenue, and as far as Morris knew it always had been. What the hell was Blakely getting at?

"It was built," Blakely continued, "on a network of underground tunnels dug-out near the turn of the eighteenth century." Blakely narrowed his weasel eyes. "*Haunted tunnels,*" he added.

Morris rolled his eyes. He didn't know if Blakely was putting him on or not, but he could certainly see where the conversation was heading. "Let me guess," he said. "It was an

Aztec burial ground, catacombs where they kept the remains of their victims hidden after they feasted on them, right?"

But Blakely shook his head. "No, no, no! It wasn't an Indian burial ground. It was a group of miners that had been sent out to search for silver. The gold rush was over by then and silver was hot. Groups of miners were hired to excavate this place by some rich prick in Tennessee who was interested in the market. Look it up in the library if you don't believe me!"

Smiling, Morris nodded. "Interesting story," he admitted. "So what happened to this band of miners? An underground explosion? Or maybe they ran into a pissed-off grizzly bear trying to hibernate? That would have been something, huh?"

Blakely was still standing in front of stall number two dressed in his gray suit and black tie. He wore spectacles (like any worthy accountant), and these he took off and began to clean on the hem of his starched shirt.

"Worse," he said. His voice dropped in a conspirator's whisper. "They got greedy is what happened. They all wanted more than their fair share of the silver and began to fight amongst themselves. Legend has it that during the melee one of them swung their pickaxe at a buddy and missed and hit a support beam, bringing the entire structure crashing down on them."

"Is that a fact?" Morris said not surprised. "So what happened?" He still wasn't sure if he was buying what Blakely was selling him, but the man had a way of being eerily convincing.

Replacing his glasses, Blakely continued: "Well...and you won't find this in any books or old transcripts...but it was rumored that one of those miners happened to survive. They say he roamed around in those dark tunnels---or what was left of them---for years, searching for an exit and eating the occasional rat, mole, or bat if he could find them. Must have been hell."

Morris's eyes widened in disbelief. "This miner survived a cave-in under tons of earth and rock?" He asked.

Blakely chuckled, slicking back his oily hair. "Does it matter, buddy?" he whispered back. "What matters is that a lot of people still think he's down there and that he's gotten lonely after all these long years and that he's looking for a playmate of some sort or someone to talk to."

"Good Lord," Morris muttered at the thought, "that must be awful." He winced as another cramp surged through his belly. He really needed to use the john, the crapper, the toilet, the shitter, whatever a person wanted to call it. His bowels were near critical mass.

"I'm sure it ain't no picnic for that miner either!" Blakely laughed. He slapped his knee and dropped Morris a knowing wink that was rather grotesque. "But you know what I think?" He asked. "If you ask me, and most people do, I think that old miner got exactly what he deserved! Yes sir!"

"Why in the world would you say such a thing!?" Morris exclaimed. His voice echoed off the tiles of the bathroom and the distant sound of a drip of water could be heard. "No one deserves such a thing!"

"C'mon, man!" Blakely said. He looked at Morris derisively. "You think this miner was some kindly old grandfather type who looked like Santa Claus and led a mule around with a pack on its back?" He shook his head. "No sir! He was probably an ornery ol' cuss who would have spit tobacco juice in your eye rather than look at you!"

And that's when Morris heard it--the hand; the hand that wore a signet ring made of gold bearing the symbol of a pyramid.

...*splish! splash! splish! splash!*...

Somehow, the tone was different this time. It wasn't a happy sound or the playful mirthfulness of a child in a bathtub full of bubbles. No. To Morris it sounded angry; something that had been pushed too far and had had enough. It was, to Morris's ear, the resonance of vengeance.

Clearing his throat, Morris took a step back. He had a clear shot to the men's room door and could run (irritable bowels or not) like the wind if necessary, but he didn't. Something was going to happen. He could feel it like the approach of a thunderstorm in late summer, at least in some respect that Blakely deserved a chance.

"Hey, James," Morris said, "I'd step away from that stall if I were you. It may not be safe."

"Why?" Blakely spun around on one brown loafer. "What are you talk—"

But by then it was too late. Morris had known it was coming---call it a premonition or that old black magic if you like---but he *had* known. The hand rose out of the toilet with a splash, seizing Blakely by the head. It shook him like a dirty rug and then began to reel him in like the world's best-dressed fish.

Blakely was squawking like a chicken, and then began to squeal, flailing at the hand with both fists. "*Jesus Christ*!!" he screamed. "What is this shit?? Get it off!! Morris!! *Get it off!!*"

But it was useless. There was nothing Morris could do but stand there watching as the strong arm of the hand pulled Blakely inside the toilet. It was fascinating.

Really.

In a macabre sort of way, like watching a particularly violent accident unfold in slow motion, the brains, the blood, the horror, all there in high-definition 3-D before your very eyes.

With a final squeal of appeal, Blakely disappeared inside stall number two. Morris had to take a look. He didn't know why---call it morbid curiosity---but he had to. He heard another splash and then, peeking around the corner of the stall, saw that Blakely was now head-first inside the toilet, his legs and feet kicking in the air as if riding an invisible bicycle. He could even hear the man gurgling beneath the water, still pleading his case. It was, in Morris's humble opinion, nothing short of *fascinating*, a once-in-a-lifetime experience.

It was a minute, maybe more, before the hand had Blakely fully submersed inside the toilet drain. Morris could only imagine the amount of force it must have taken---*the power that the hand must have*---to have squeezed Blakely's body into such a narrow passage. It was a sickening idea, the water clouding in swirls of blackish-red blood and then, like a cork, one of Blakely's blue-colored eyes appeared floating on the surface. It bobbed there for a moment, staring at Morris.

Why me??? The eye screamed at him. *Why me*?? *What did I ever do to you*??

Plenty, Morris thought, and flushed it away. Turning, he unbuckled his pants, ready to relieve his aching bowels. He felt safer now, more secure, as if the hand and he had bonded in some sort of unholy communion. And as if to solidify this line of reasoning, Morris noticed something lying at the bottom of the toilet bowl, something that hadn't been flushed down.

With a steady hand, Morris reached in and retrieved the object. It was the gold ring-the signet ring with a pyramid in its center. It was the hand's ring. He turned it over in his palm, studying it. *A gift?* He thought. *A gift from the hand? Were things like this even possible?* Perhaps he was on the verge of a mental breakdown or maybe a blood clot had broken loose and gone to his brain?

Morris shook his head. Probably not. More than likely the ring had slipped off and—

When an idea struck him. In fact, it was more than an idea now...it was a *certainty*. The hand wasn't to be feared, he realized. But how could he *really be* certain? How could he convince himself that the ring meant something and wasn't an object of mere coincidence that had dropped into his lap? *It was impossible! Not after what he'd witnessed! Poor Blakely! King turd of the toilet bowl now!* He almost giggled but didn't dare.

Instead, Morris slipped the ring over his index finger, the exact same finger the hand had worn it on. It fit perfectly and felt warm to the touch. Somehow, Morris had known it would. The ring was his, but for how long? There was really no way of telling, and Morris didn't have the time to speculate. In short, he needed to excavate his own bowels and the time had come, ready or not.

Quickly, and with the grim smile of a man on the verge of a heart attack, Morris buckled his pants and exited the men's room. The door swished silently shut as he made his way down a narrow corridor. He took a sharp right at the first corner, and then down the stairs at a trot to the double-doors that led outside where the sun was out and the traffic snarled with noon-time motorists. He would crap in the alley between the buildings if necessary and think things over; stir them around inside the cauldron boiling in his mind and see what popped-up.

Could the hand be trusted? Morris asked himself, as he entered the shadows of the alley. It was cool here, and comforting, a place where dirty things were meant to happen and he immediately began to unbuckle his trousers again as his stomach gave a final and demanding ultimatum: *Shit or die!*

Morris bent to the will of nature, his legs trembling in anticipation, and he thought out loud without realizing it, "Perhaps it can," he grunted. He felt a flush of momentary shame pass over him at what he was being forced to do, but dismissed it. ???

"Perhaps it can," Morris repeated to the alley. "And perhaps it can't. I'll have to wait; I'll have to see what happens and then go from there. That's what I'll do." His eyes brightened and his gut felt lighter. "Yeah, I'll wait and see what happens to the others and then decide from there."

Morris smiled at his decision and, although it meant avoiding the crapper for fear of the worst (or for the simple fear of nothing at all), he was happy and thought of things that were yet (or not yet) to come.

Like Mr. Carlson for instance, with his no-bullshit policy and his circa 1950's burr haircut. He wondered if Mr. Carlson would "get to the bottom of things" with the hand present? He had no doubt that he would.

And there were others at Leviathan Printing that might need attention. Morris stood tentatively waiting for another explosive outburst from his bowels, and when it didn't happen, he smiled in relief and worked his trousers back up to his waist.

Or what about the janitor? Morris suddenly thought. Mr. What's-His-Name with the hair sprouting out of his ears? The man who insisted on smoking cheap, smelly cigars in the break room and stank of stale bourbon most times. He could *certainly* use an adjustment.

And the list went on, and on, and on, and Morris would remember the names in the days that followed and kept a diary of the outcome as the events unfolded. And perhaps someday, maybe, and when Morris had his irritable bowels under control and the planets were aligned in the universe in their correct order, Morris would take a trip upstairs to the men's room and visit the hand. They'd talk, and maybe have a laugh or two.

Maybe.

The End.

SPECTROPHOBIA

By Tracey Chapman

"Sergeant Roscoe what have we got?"

"Over here chief this is how they found her."

"My God, was she thrown through the glass?"

"No chief, a passerby said she ran at the window, screaming, acting, what was it now? Like a monkey."

The glass cascaded down the stairs in glistening fragments. Amy sat at the top, uncontrollable tears streaming down her face. Fear, not of seven years bad luck but of the imprisonment of her reflection.

Her house was cast aside of anything with a view – dark and expressionless but to Amy – heaven. These four walls were her life and had been that way for nearly ten years. She had tried many times stepping outside that front door, but it wasn't fear of the world that held her a recluse just its mirrored mazes and reflective conundrums.

Her life was like a revolving door spinning, just constantly spinning. She had no one here for her anymore after her parents had died in a freak boating accident. If only she could have plucked up the courage to let go, all of this pain could have vanished, sunk 4,000 feet down off the coast of

Portugal. No more voices, no more screaming just the solitude of the ocean around her.

Friends had tried everything, planning routes, avoiding awkward social interaction but the years drifted away. One by one, twenty friends soon became two, then— none. Exhausted of all options, Amy found herself alone.

Amy sat motionless staring down into the darkness of the morning. Should she clear it up now, what was the point, it's not like she was going anywhere. Amy paused for a second and sniffed the air. An all too familiar smell was wafting through from next door. What was that? Muffins, freshly baked banana muffins.

"Hey look! It's monkey girl." laughter echoed down the vast corridor. She was there again at St Luke's Academy for girls where her vital teenage years were taken from her through torment and ridicule.

Her parents had been unwilling to help her "work your way through it girl. It will toughen you up." Needless pain and suffering "Hey monkey girl, got any muffins? Banana muffins."

"Muffins, muffins…." Amy winces in pain, Blood flows down her arm in little rivulets the shard fell from her fingers and bounced down the stairs. The shock of pain brought her back to reality.

Irrational Fears

Self-harming had become Amy's release. The scars, little ridges etched into her skin like mementos. A collection of accomplishments giving her a sense of pride, just not the type you brag about. "Hey look at this one. It's from the photo frame. What a picture!" My God, I'm even more of a freak. In Amy's self-conscious state, she hardly heard the chime of the doorbell reverberating down the hallway. The second ring was more piercing, Amy turned in disbelief no one had rung her doorbell in years.

Amy cautiously approached the door her heart pounding, she knelt down and slowly opened the letterbox. On her brief glance, a wave of relief flowed through her body it must have been her imagination. It came again the loud echoing knock sent her sprawling backwards a women's voice floated through the letterbox "Amy, Amy Johnson I know you're in there come on its freezing out here."

Miranda was getting to the point now of jogging on the spot when she noticed the door slightly ajar "Who are you?" Amy adjusted her eyes to the brightness of the day.

"It's Miranda you know, can we talk about it indoors my fingers are turning to icicles."

Miranda squeezed her way in trying not to show any expression of the dark gloomy interior she had just entered.

"Wow, it's interesting what you've done with the place." The sarcastic undertones in Miranda's voice washed over Amy who was retreating towards the kitchen. "I was saddened by the news of your parents, your mum rang me years back but I was heading out to Australia and…"

"Why?" Miranda hadn't heard the response. Her concentration diverted to the shattered glass strewn across the stairs with droplets of blood scattered in-between. "Why did my mum ring you?"

Miranda couldn't believe someone could live in such chaos and disarray. "You know, I think she just wanted me to check in on you."

"Oh did she pass responsibility because she was too ashamed to come herself?"

"Look, it's really none of my business." Amy could sense Miranda's awkwardness and her own anger rising within.

She could have been born into a normal family but no, if being mixed race wasn't enough she was put through regimental training to toughen her up, when all Amy really wanted was to be loved, to be told she belonged. Her parents had been devoid of any affection bringing her up as only they knew how. But at what cost? Her life, her family, her sanity?

Amy still couldn't remember who Miranda was or why now she had decided to be a part of her life again. She kept going over and over in her head the way she had made her way into the house. "It's Miranda, you know." Like that was supposed to help in some way.

"We really should get this glass cleared up, open a few curtains, and then go out for a stroll." Miranda had crunched through that glass for the last time.

"What do you want? You come into my house, expecting me to know you. "

"You don't remember me and that hurts." A wry smile crossed Miranda's lips. She had edged her way farther along into the living room.

"What do you want?" Amy was finding herself becoming more tense and nervous, following Miranda along like a little lost puppy.

"You know it really is beautiful outside, great for maybe swinging in the trees, having a banana." Miranda grabbed the curtains and flung them open. The light flooded the living room while Amy stood frozen to the spot.

"Remember me now?" Miranda whispered into Amy's ear.

St Luke's Academy bathroom, she had been that girl, images swirled around Amy's head. She felt dizzy then sick, and the piercing scream that followed seemed like an out-of-body experience. Amy remembered. A shocked Miranda knew it and stumbled backwards.

Amy grabbed for the chair with her eyes fixed in rage and flung it with force straight at the ornate bay windows. The glass erupted around them in shimmering fragments.

An eerie silence fell over the house. Miranda lay motionless on the floor, a seeping pool of blood surrounding her body. Amy's gaze was still focused on the shattered window while a lady from across the street had heard all the commotion and made her way towards the property. Amy sensed a presence. Was the lady was staring at her? Amy's expression changed as she rubbed at her eyes, was she hallucinating? A rage so strong flowed through her body. She sprinted to the front door slamming it back with such force, it ricocheted off the wall, the innocent lady stood no chance. Amy bowled into her full force sending her hurtling backwards down the stone steps snapping her neck as she fell.

Amy looked down at the lady. "You did this to me. All I ever wanted was to be loved." The tears flowed down her cheeks. The realization that she was outside quickly dawned upon her. She looked up and saw the shattered front window, the blood spattered across her t-shirt, and the lady lying at her feet not moving. Why was the lady or Amy? there? God, what had she done? A stranger's voice echoed from across the street "Miss, miss is everything ok?"

Amy turned suddenly with panic surging through her body. She couldn't think clearly, because it had all happened so fast, everything was a blur. Her body swiveled, her legs started to jog, and before she knew it she was at a full sprint down the street not daring to look back. "Miss, "the stranger's voice carried away on the cool breeze.

The street was amass with busy afternoon shoppers. Amy had run into her own worst nightmare wall-to-wall mirrors. She tried to calm herself. Her heart was pounding out of her chest. How had one day gone so horribly wrong? She sat herself down on a nearby bench and closed her eyes, wanting it all to go away, willing it, her head was spinning, and in her subconscious, she heard them. The voices were back. "Monkey girl, hey monkey girl" "give us a banana go on." Amy's eyes popped wide open as she felt the eyes of the entire street upon her.

"Make it stop, please, make it stop!" It was as if Amy was pleading with everyone around her but no one looked her way. A brief glance upwards and she caught her reflection in the window. Before she could control it or make sense of it, a loud piercing howl came from within her.

She stood tall now on the bench and shouted to anyone who was near. "I see it now, you were right."

A second blood-curdling howl halted the shoppers in their tracks. Amy positioned herself like a monkey on all fours and hurtled towards the shop window, pouncing at the last minute before anyone could do anything. She smashed through the glass with such velocity that the window imploded outwards spraying shoppers with shards of glass. She fell limp like a ragdoll.

It was over.

Tutu Much

By DJ Tyrer

Ballerinaphobia? Is that a word? Can you just slap –phobia on the end of any word? I guess it doesn't matter. Maybe there's a proper term like coulrophobia for clowns. Now, coulrophobia, that makes sense. If you think about it, clowns *are* scary- painted faces like a criminal's disguise… leering grins or mournful frowns… acts that are based on violence and humiliation… psychopaths that favour the outfit? It's no wonder people are scared of them. Indeed, it's supposed to be very common. You have to wonder where they can find an audience. Tell someone you're afraid of clowns and they'll understand but tell them you're scared of ballerinas and they'll laugh at you.

I can't really blame them; I don't really understand why they scare me either, I just know they do. I've tried to find an explanation for it – something to do with them being so thin, perhaps, or the movements they make when dancing – but none of it rings true. After all, if it was because they are thin, why does nobody else equally skinny bother me? And if it was the dance, then the male ballet dancers would surely upset me too but they don't. I cannot recall nor have I been told of any early trauma involving a ballerina that could be at the root of my problem. No, my fear is utterly irrational and as odd a phobia as they come.

Now, in general terms, a fear of ballerinas isn't exactly debilitating. After all, the world is full of people who would never go to see a ballet yet are not reduced to gibbering wrecks by the dancers. Ballerinas are not exactly common on TV either. Thus, from a practical point of view, the phobia had little impact on my life. Okay, I couldn't watch *Black Swan*, but it otherwise has been easy to cope with in the normal course of life. That morning, however, wasn't normal. It was anything but normal.

It all began like just another ordinary day. Of course, that's the thing about such outrageous twists of fate: you never see them coming. In fiction, there would be foreshadowing. In reality, they ambush you. One moment everything seems to be, as it should then your life is changed forever.

Yes, it all began like just any other day, but I was deposited into my own personal hell somewhere on the High Street between Starbucks and Nandos. Ballerinas.

What were ballerinas doing there? I'm not entirely certain. It doesn't really matter, anyway.

All that matters is that some ten or twelve ballerinas appeared out of a space between two empty shops. Where they came from and where they were going, I have no idea. Maybe it was something to do with charity, or maybe they were going to or from a dance class. All that matters is they were there.

I halted in mid step, frozen in terror.

One of the ballerinas stopped and turned to look at me. She raised a hand and gave me a little wave accompanied by the loveliest smile I've ever seen. At least it would've been had it not belonged to a ballerina. Whenever I close my eyes, I can still see that smile. So kind, so benevolent, so hideously entwined with the thing I so singularly loath, fear, and most of all, presaging disaster.

Rather than the endearment the gesture was doubtless intended to evoke, it sent a further frisson of fear through me as if it were the grin of a predator, and I let out a shriek and turned and ran.

Straight into the road.

Straight into the path of a minicab.

I went straight up over the bonnet and roof and, then, lost consciousness. This was something of a relief, given the state of terror I was in. Then the ballerinas came running to check my condition.

***

"How are you feeling?" asked a pleasantly soft and concerned-sounding voice as I drifted back to consciousness.

"Mum?" I asked, which was a silly thing to say was given she'd been dead for years.

The voice chuckled musically. "No... it's me." That didn't help as I didn't recognise her voice and I still had my eyes shut. "I felt so guilty; I just had to come check to see how you are. I blame myself," she added.

That made sense when I opened my eyes and saw a face I recognised gazing down at me—the ballerina. A second later, I took the rest of her in, saw she was still in costume, and WHO? Half-leapt, half-rolled to one side with a cry, falling so that my feet were on the bed and my head was smacked into the door of the bedside cabinet.

"Oh, dear!" she cried and ran round the bed, doubtless intending to help me.

Clearly seeing the whole of her, however, merely caused me to shriek and swing my feet from the bed to kick her.

She fell with a cry and I grabbed hold of the bed to drag myself to my feet. I was still in a state of frenzied agitation as she gazed up at me in bewilderment.

She lay there before me, stunned, and the primal urges of flight or fight battled inside me. Fight won out and I began to kick and stamp at her while roaring in terror.

She was screaming too and her cries were joined by those of one of her friends who stepped into the room to see what was happening. Like the first ballerina, she was between the door, and me allowing fight to take control once again. Despite my terror of her, I grabbed a bedpan left lying atop the cabinet and lunged at her, swinging with all my strength.

With a horrible crack, her head snapped sideways and she fell to the floor, her wide eyes matching my own.

I jumped over her and ran out of the room screaming, shoving aside anyone who got in my way.

It took two policemen to restrain me, and a nurse to sedate me. Gratefully, I embraced the darkness.

***

When I next awoke, I was here strapped to a bed and awaiting assessment. I'd killed two innocent women. You can imagine the horror I felt! I never intended to do it. I was maddened with fear. I would give anything to undo what I had done. But, their blood is upon me, nonetheless.

Of course, they have no intention of letting me go. Madness is not much of a defense. It could keep me from prison but would then keep me here. Besides, they tell me I am rational now and will remain so as long as I avoid seeing a ballerina.

So, next I am to stand trial.

Now I find myself contemplating an all-too-rational fear of men in wigs and red robes...

Irrational Fears

I feel as powerless as ever I did when confronted by a ballerina... but at least in prison I'll never have to see one again...

LIKE WHISPERS

By Alex Harasymiw

It is with great difficulty that I pen this letter, least of all, perhaps, because only a carefully guarded supply of sandwich wrappers may serve in place of paper. Shoeless amidst a cold, aluminum bench, a cold, aluminum toilet, and high and low steel bars trapping both perspective and prospective escape, I have seen all those things that once made me who I am march back and forth on the other side, out of reach. Still, I find I must explain myself to you, even if you no longer wish to listen. Over and against our love of yelling at each other's familiar faces, I situate the wellbeing of our son, a sentiment so haunting that it slips through even these steel bars, and out of necessity, fills my cell with its fog.

We were seated, you and I, decked out in our silent, Sunday's best while our respective lawyers partitioned all that was left of our marriage: the car, the house, my pension, our child, the sofa. The office overlooked those orderly maple husks and well-spaced benches where we first met, and subsequently, came to variously love one another. Such was our dislocation, however, that I found the discussion of our shared history scarcely required my participation at all, and under the pretense of another smoke-break, I gathered my things and escaped into the town. You should remember the day so far, even if you will never understand.

I wandered from the town centre, more following whimsy, slushy melt-water than any other street sign. When I finally looked up from the ground, I noticed the dim, winter sun had given way to darkness, and I was, despite my long acquaintance with this town, lost in the disorienting sameness of a shadowy subdivision. The long-tall houses crowded out all avenues of escape; wet snow cemented in the cold, immortalizing the past paths of others' homes while denying my own walk a similar impression. As it was, I despaired the thought of checking my phone for a map, knowing full well what other messages awaited me.

I drifted aimlessly, stopping, searching for a route that would keep me from coming around full circle. Eventually, after the course of an immeasurable amount of time, I spied a narrow alley between two houses, which opened out on a dark clearing. A low bench reached out to me from beneath its icy skin, shrinking my arms into their jacket, and tucking my chin snug under its collar. Hoping to rest a while before continuing, I closed my eyes against that cold and weary trek. I must have fallen asleep, though, because when I opened them again, a dense squall had taken hold, forming little snow dunes on the creases of my lap.

Lampposts sputtered on and I could see harsh, rectangular windows hovering ominously off to the sides, dimly revealing what seemed to be an infinitely long and desolate valley. The ground looked to be uniformly flat with no visible walkways. The cold air, still retaining some of the day's dampness, drenched my bones and sweated up my nose with snot. However, for all these discomforts, it was the supreme, depthless appearance of the place that most filled me with singular feelings of strange foreboding; for peeking out from the jacket's neck, crunching up all foetal in its womb, it was impossible to make out any distinction between the ground and the sky in the sheer, all-consuming whiteness. Indeed, if it were not for my previous approach, of which only a vague reminiscence remained, I would have been utterly incapacitated before this drop-off into oblivion.

Innumerable aromas of roast chicken, steak, and pizza mingled tantalizingly in the air, each enjoyable in isolation, but cruel and oppressive when they washed over me at dinner's high tide. It was at this point that I noticed, while my mind cooked its own, decadent meal, that I had been subconsciously shovelling snow into my mouth at an appalling rate. Whatever heat I had been afforded beneath the tent-like jacket had been

102

completely extinguished. So it was, the demands of hunger tinged with cold prepared me for the journey.

I untucked my legs and began testing the snow with my feet. As the stuff clung to my pants and spilled over the sides of my shoes, I considered my position. It seemed more than likely that I was in some kind of park, and if it did truly extend as far as the suggestion of the windows, perhaps it is a soccer field. In which case, there ought to be some kind of parking lot on the other side and further off, a road out of this thoroughly blinding neighbourhood; or so I thought, considering convenience and economy to have been the architect's impetus.

I had originally thought that, with a few, strategic bounds, I might spare my feet from the worst of the freshly fallen snow, but the gesture proved futile as an imperceptible base layer of those frozen footprints threatened to twist me around each time I unknowingly slipped my own feet into their grooves. In this way, I was reduced to a sort of acrobat's shuffle, awkwardly shifting about as my socks turned from wet to frozen. The constant, throbbing pain was almost unbearable, and whenever I jammed a toe against this or that buried object, it sent a wave of nausea shooting through my body. And still the procession of lights flanked me on both sides. Their only comfort was the certainty of my course; knowing where exactly

I was forbidden, and reminding me into what frigid darkness I must travel.

When I eventually spied a faint light on my horizon, much higher and more central than the rest, emerge from between the rows, my pursuit of it became feverish. My reckless gait was punished with frequent falls and wrenched ankles. I cannot recall what thoughts exactly must have possessed me just then. It was as though some primal thing had taken hold, and I was forced to watch as it lurched heedlessly after an alien, ephemeral hope; again, what hope exactly, I cannot say. Without any pretense to foresight, I can tell you, however, that when I was able to shake myself of that beastly trance, I found myself crouched in the lee of a plastic wall, beneath what I took to be an unusually tall lamppost, pocking the sky above with a sickly, yellow blemish.

Immense pain wracked my body; cold sweat froze on my face; hot blood stuck flesh and fabric together, pain ripping through my guts at the least movement. I still had the presence of mind, at the time, to see that my injuries were relatively minor and might be readily treated with bandages, warm food, and sleep. This knowledge only compounded the torture, knowing that no more than a short walk to the left or right a family, just like ours, could have laughed the pain away, convalescing as winter's chokehold melted to steam in their fireplace.

It had been foolish to run so carelessly.

I still beat myself up over those self-inflicted wounds.

Finding it impossible to rest any longer, I helped myself to my feet with the aid of the plastic wall, but in the end, crashed through this feeble crutch when my full weight leaned against it. I screamed in frustration, eyes shut tight in agony, tears streaming as far as their meager heat could carry them. The pain was intolerable, and I resigned myself to die there, caught out in that space between the houses, a pathetic, lonely, wretched waste.

Then a sudden wave of heat, warmth even, crept up from my toes, thawing my eyelids with its strange comfort. I felt for the ground with my fingers and found it to be smooth as glass, my tips now registering the minutest of nicks and chips despoiling its otherwise flawless surface. All around the low hum of propane heaters, standing tall and dense as trees, reverberated from the plastic, brightly coloured barriers of the perimeter, like a Gregorian choir. No snow touched the ground here, save that trickling in from my entrance. I was surprised to see the whole area, from end to end, clear as a fluorescent summer day, bathing in what seemed a light sun shower. A somewhat medieval, castle-like playground sat on a small hillock in the distance, resplendent in glittering ice amidst the veritable rink surrounding it, imperious in spite of the squall beyond its walls.

I do not know what powers decided to put propane heaters in a children's playground, nor what reason or negligence had left them on into the night. I could see, however, it had had a peculiar effect on the snow, melting the stuff as it fell into a near-tropical rainfall. Then as it touched a surface, it was refreezing and coating everything in thick ice. My clothes became wet with sweat and rain, but this did nothing to deter the overall sensation of disquieting warmth.

Despite the vague, inexplicable uneasiness I felt in my new situation, the clarity I was afforded did much to steady my thoughts. The heat had fortified my limbs to the point where I was confident in ascending the hill. From there I believed I could gauge just how much more of that seemingly infinite stretch of park was left to travel, and prepare myself accordingly. If necessary, it might also be possible to take shelter in some roofed area of the playground for the night, though I was, loathe to consider this option at all.

The ascent proved to be of little difficulty and it was not long before I reached a small hut beside the playground, a playhouse, or mock-convenience store of some sort. For a moment, I took shelter there from the rain, fishing my cigarettes out of a pocket, only to notice that they would become hopelessly drenched. I vividly remember looking out from the window as I crouched awkwardly beneath the building's low roof. What I saw was astonishing: it was as though some wretched parody of human existence had been plopped down on earth to spite our hubris, our claims to progress, meaning, and importance. Little play-jeeps idled, forever rooted to the ground by thick metal poles heedless of vain appeals to the accelerator and steering wheel; sea-creatures too, seals, whales, and sharks creaked eerily back and forth. Rusted handlebars plunged deep into their skulls, betraying their clownish grins and dilated pupils as the frozen contortions of pain, humiliation, and despair that they were; a spinning wheel where one might sit, drunk off speed, blind to the fact that no matter how fast one goes, no destination will ever be reached beyond that eternal cycle. Never before had I felt my life as small and insignificant as when I stared out at those miniature caricatures.

Needless to say, any semblance of rest alluded me, and I resolved to finish my climb and break out of that nightmare world as quickly as possible. A gradual ramp covered with rubber tires seemed the most salliable aspect of the fort, so from there I decided to attempt the summit, even though this route would bring me unnervingly close to the simian obstacle-poles. This incline terminated in a short, hemmed-in plateau, a barely perceptible layer of ice coating its floor. It was now possible, however, to spy a definite route to the perch I had striven for, and so with the same acrobatic shuffle I had employed throughout my journey thus far, I traversed a drooping suspension bridge, which shuddered before my footfalls as it shrugged its icy coat off into the unfathomable void below. Not long after I found myself atop the castle's eminence, and was afforded my first, disparaging glimpse of just what lay ahead.

Not only was the fury of the squall continuing unabated beyond the walls, but also much to my horror, I noticed that the window lights that'd guided my passage thus far had begun to shut off all around me. It was as if any hope of steady navigation through the night was extinguished with a bedtime-kiss.

It was in this moment of utter resignation that I saw it; my body went stiff and I stood, paralyzed with fright. In my peripherals, I detected two large, unblinking eyes staring through me, no more than half a meter to my left. Whatever it was, I was at its mercy. I think it was this overriding sense of futility that gave me the courage for what I did next. In an instant, I spun around to face it, thinking a sudden shock would cause it to recoil, but I only managed to slip on the ice, falling on my back before its monolithic form. The thing towered over me, clenched fists poised, grotesquely deformed head motionless, eyes, strangely enough, still fixed on the point in space where I had previously been standing. Though further details were obscured by deep shadow, I gradually deduced that the thing was, for now, inert. Regardless, the lack of imminent attack did little to quell my overriding sense of dread. It was still uncertain whom or for what sinister purpose the thing had been constructed, if it had not in fact merely sprung into being from some otherworldly hell.

This curiosity soon overcame my fear, however great it was, and I worked myself back up onto my tentative feet, feeling like a child beneath a magnifying glass. Standing in the thing's shadow, my eyes were able to adjust more securely to the lowlight, allowing for a more detailed examination. Barely discernable beneath its icy gloss, I could make out a faint, yellowish tinge, which betrayed the thing, along with its bent, curving top, as a shape distinctly, and strangely, banana-like. The disturbingly large fists I had seen before still menaced me from its flanks, but in addition to what I had seen before, two sardonic thumbs jutted skywards from their respective hands. Animating what by all learned accounts shouldn't be considered a face, but was, a malicious grin with two, hideously elongated teeth, one on the top, one on the bottom of what I hesitate to call a mouth, were barred indiscriminately at its surroundings, just as its eyes seemed to take in everything and nothing. I could not help sensing something peculiarly apish in the frozen grimace, though I know now that this is an absurd observation. There were also a number of crude markings, letters and pictures, on and around the thing. Something like permanent marker, distorted and nearly illegible lie beneath its cold, wavering surface.

It is difficult to describe just how intensely fascinating I found these markings at the time. I believed in no small way, their import lay in the context they might provide, metaphorically presented or otherwise, for the uncanny situation of the place, as well as the object they were scrawled upon. Indeed, I have since become so lost to them that it is really only their faint memory that sustains me anymore.

As I have mentioned, the primeval words were barely legible, but I believe that they were intended to exhibit the names, familiar or personal, of those who had come to the site. Perhaps they were a part of some kind of aeon-old pilgrimage. This I deduced by examining the penmanship, variously stylized and without any ready pattern in word content. Nor were the messages particularly long, usually being but a single marking, a full stop, and a brief series of characters. Some were even overlaid, suggesting a sort of contest whereby one's ruinous neglect of the ritual was superseded by more pious and regular personages, and so a sort of attendance recorded there; for whose eyes, though, I cannot say.

The pictures, disturbingly vivid and iconic, shed any doubt as to the religious nature of the idol I beheld. Countless drawings were of a similar fixation, though the varying nature of the illustrations pointed to several participants, rather than one, master craftsman in the tribe. The objects in question were much like the idol they were written upon, with that same banana shape. Only instead of tapering off at the end, one side appeared to terminate in two, bulbous orbs at times disproportionately sized in comparison to the thing that stood before me. There was little to hint at what the pictures symbolized. A literal translation would be similarly lacking, for although the pictures did indeed bear a striking resemblance to the thing, they possessed a startlingly monstrous scale next to more familiar, pictorial depictions that I made out. They were such things as horses, trees, men, and perhaps most disturbing of all, cars, spaceships, and skyscrapers. These more modern inclusions, alongside one picture in particular, that of the aforementioned thing penetrating some sort of wispy veil, suggested to me that whatever strange cult was responsible still kept up its activities into the present time, though I reserved in my mind, for sanity's sake, the possibility that the images were merely the apocryphal inclusions of other hapless travelers like myself. I just so happened to have a permanent marker of my own from our meeting earlier in the day, and though I cannot exactly explain the impulse, I felt a curious urge to write my own name down.

No sooner had I chipped away a section of ice and crouched to add my mark than a sudden rush of wind shot past my shoulder. In addition to this shock, a gradually diminishing scream could be heard emanating from the idol, accompanied by a horrific thumping. I started to back away from the banana-thing, but soon found my escape anticipated by something especially cold. When I spun my head around at the unexpected obstacle, I could see that what I had brushed against was not the wall of the perch, but a pair of stiff legs. Looking up further in awe, I could clearly make out the loathsome creature to which they belonged. Pallid skin pulled back from sunken eyes, skin pale of pigmentation and nearly translucent, decked out in a suit that only emphasized its hideously alien nature, with an unwavering stare, it stood there and looked deep into the eyes of the idol. It did not seem to notice me at all. It stepped back only to be replaced by another, this one carrying a small child, reminiscent of the way one might handle an old bowling trophy. Despite being bundled heavily against the weather, there was no doubt in my mind that what I now call a child was in fact human. Unlike its spellbound captor, the boy caught my eye with an expression of bleak despair not easily forgotten.

With a haste, I would have thought it incapable of; the creature cocked back its arm and shunted the boy into the center of the banana-idol. A thin scream resounded as the child disappeared into a vacuous portal. I scrambled backward towards the low barrier of the perch, and despite my frantic kicking, made painfully slow progress over the ice. As I readied myself to vault the ledge, I spared a look over my shoulder. One of the creatures crouched apart from the mob, etching something on the banana-idol with the marker I then realized I had dropped. An inexplicable feeling of anguish wracked my body, and I tumbled over the edge. The last thing I remember with any confidence is hearing a pitched wailing, as of a thousand children at once, explode from the idol. Upon hitting the ground, the sound slowly succumbing to the hum of the propane heaters.

The rest is lost to me. I vaguely recall lurching through the snow and shambling over a wooden fence. From there only the crashing of glass and a violent whirling motion, there was an odd feeling of being carried off somewhere, and the faint smell of leather and coffee; some lights, blue and red; a maddening siren trapped inside my head.

Irrational Fears

When at last I clawed my way back to reality, it was to find myself in the hospital on Front Street, strapped down and bandaged up. My feet, they said, had been stricken with frostbite, and that my wild flailing had prevented paramedics from treating them on the way over. They had been amputated earlier in the week.

Few to whom I have told my tale are patient enough to listen all the way through, and I have frequently been warned against telling it at all due to my excitability. When I became more stable, I was transferred to the local police station, and am presently being held here on charges I scarcely understand. The more I plead innocence, the guiltier I am found. I hoped to call you, but my appeal was denied; I hoped to send a previous letter to you through my lawyer, but I believe he is withholding it for his own, nefarious gain.

It's when the air is humid and the damp, winter fog rolls in through these bars; that is when I remember. I see the thing, the banana-idol; its grin, those eyes; my name engraved forever on its surface as though on a tombstone; God, those eyes!

I have done everything I can to dispel the vision, though I am not capable of very much anymore. I know that nothing I say or write will sway you any longer; that much is clear. Our son may be too young to be curious about my disappearance, but one day he will be. You must tell him everything I have told you. Better yet, save these sandwich wrappers, give them to him when he is ready. He must know, he has a right to know; he must not make the same mistakes I did. This is the last thing I will ask of you. The rest already belongs to you anyway.

Sometimes I wonder if things could have turned out differently. I wonder if the account I have given was ever anything more than an exhausted hallucination or a dream lived out too long. But then, nothing in my present suggests that this is the case, and it would be my and our son's, utter ruin were I too weak to plead it myself. This I maintain, if nothing else.

I still see those loathsome pilgrims. In my dreams, I see all the children of the world gathered up in the arms of that hideously self-serving ritual. I see them chucked anxiously into the flames of a thousand banana-idols, their little screams burning down to ash and returning them as those same pilgrims, until at last the earth is nothing more than a frigid waste, an empty shell, our snow-covered footprints, the grinning mask of a thousand banana-idols.

There is not much room left; my sandwich wrappers are nearly exhausted. All that is left is to trust that my mail carrier will bring this letter to you, and that you still live in my house. If it is as I believe, and you truly cannot bring yourself to ever let our boy see me, then promise me; never take him to that space between the houses.

Yours,

The Other Side of the Door

By David Bergheim

The sound of knocking draws uncomfortable feelings back to the surface. I am reminded of the victims, and how the simple act of greeting the wrong stranger can turn an ordinary day into the last. The logical part of my brain tells me it's safe to open the door now, but I just can't shake the sense that something bad could happen if I do.

My job with the city gives me access to people inside the investigation, including the lead detective, Paul Muldowney. We went to high school together, and we often get together after work to have a beer and talk. Mostly, he does the drinking while I listen to him vent his frustration about the cunning killer who has dodged and eluded his grasp.

After the third body was found, he shared his suspicion that someone who makes deliveries for a living was committing the murders. A witness saw a man in a crisply pressed uniform carrying a box as he approached the victim's front door. When the body was found wrapped in packaging tape, the profile of a deranged deliveryman who hunted women started to make sense to Paul.

He told me that the killer was taking souvenirs from his victims. Locks of hair were always cut off, along with an ear and sometimes a finger or toe as well. It sounds gruesome, I know, but it makes sense if you think about it. A criminal profiler theorized the killer was collecting the parts so he could relive his crimes long after the bodies were disposed of.

Paul felt like he was close to catching the guy, but then the killer threw detectives for a loop. The fourth victim -- this time a man -- was found with a different type of binding. The body was displayed more grotesquely than the others were, with a hand cupped to its missing ear as if trying to listen to a clue that investigators couldn't hear.

The police held this and other gory details back from the press because they didn't want to give the killer the satisfaction of terrorizing the public. But secrets can only be kept for so long, and the whispers grew louder as more information leaked out. The media reported the early deaths as routine murders, but after the fifth body was recovered, they realized that a serial killer was prowling the city.

Their reporting began to follow a pattern as distinctive as the killer's did. Stories of missing people that the press mostly yawned at before the rampage suddenly become big news. Intense coverage ensued as panicked loved ones and friends held vigils and prayed for a safe return. But after a few days, those hopes would be dashed by the discovery of a partially intact body, dramatically posed to maximize the horror.

The victims were always found in a natural setting, in a meadow with sunflowers in one case, and next to a wheat field outside the city in another. The serenity surrounding the still, lifeless body served as a stark contrast to the terror unleashed when a knock on the door was answered.

I recall watching the television as a reporter stood in front of a park, pointing to where the sixth body was found in a bed of irises. She breathlessly retold some of what had been learned from the police, with more than a hint of disquiet beneath the surface. Like me, the reporter knew more about the murders than she could say in public, and viewers picked up on the vibe.

The bubble of invincibility -- that feeling of having immunity against really bad things -- had popped, and there was an ominous feeling in the air that life could quickly come to an end for anybody who answered a knock on the door. As the public lost faith in the city's ability to protect them, the mayor leaned heavily on the chief of police to find answers. In turn, the pressure was passed down the chain of command until the nearly impossible weight rested squarely on Paul's shoulders.

Sales of deadbolt locks and alarm systems soared. There was a misguided belief that adding more layers of armor could keep the predator from entering, when in reality the killer was luring people outside the safety of their homes. And there was nothing that could have protected the victims once they were under his control. I suppose that a false sense of security is better than having none at all, but the killings continued unabated despite all the precautions being taken to ward off the unwanted stranger.

The knocking I hear on the door now brings those memories back. Perhaps it would have been a reasonable precaution to install a peephole when the killings started. I am normally cool under pressure, but it bothers me that I can't see who is on the other side of the door.

The news media decided that it would help if they named the menace who was boosting their ratings, and they floated several monikers before one finally stuck. When a security camera captured grainy images of the seventh unlucky victim being lured away from a yellow house, the mysterious stranger was given the label "The Door Knocker Killer."

Paul had hoped that the video would provide a big break in the case, but it only served to heighten the community's fear. The front of the suspect's head was not fully detected by the camera, and even NASA's most advanced photographic manipulation software couldn't reveal a face so heavily cast in shadows. The original theory that the man was a delivery driver was scrapped when the images revealed that the killer was wearing a different type of uniform.

It was a bad day for Paul when pictures came back from the video lab clearly showing a police department patch on the subject's shoulder. We met at a cafe that night and sat on the terrace speculating about which members of the force might be capable of committing such crimes. I proposed the names of a few officers I particularly dislike, but Paul was having a hard time believing that the Door Knocker Killer might be someone so close to him.

Faced with the very real possibility that a man in blue, the department felt it could no longer hold back details of the crimes, was committing the murders. As a precaution, the police paired up officers and instructed the public not to answer if a single policeman knocked on their door. It was a necessary step, I suppose, but the wary city cringed at the thought that even police on the street couldn't be trusted.

Reporters soon revealed that the killer was using a wide range of tools to accomplish his means. Pliers. Clippers. Saws. Hammers. All such common items that they were untraceable to a single hardware store where a purchase might have been recorded. By the time of the tenth murder, a hatchet and different types of knives had been added to the list, and the crescendo of fear built as each new instrument was introduced.

Some elements of the picture remained constant. Traces of bleach and other cleansers were found on each of the recovered victims, and it appeared that the bodies had been scrubbed to remove clues before they were disposed of. But the amount of residue left increased significantly from the eighth victim on. The grainy security video had also allowed police to identify another consistency. The eyewitness from the third murder had described the delivery driver as a man of medium height and medium build and that squared with the size of the policeman who appeared at the seventh victim's door. This detail enabled investigators to exclude a few suspects, though it offered little additional help.

When a newspaper reported this fact, the killer's description proved to be just vague enough to bring half the men in the city under suspicion. The fabric of the community frayed further under the strain of distrust, and I too could feel the uncomfortable gaze of strangers appraising the risk I posed when I walked down the street.

This heightened sense of suspicion generated several leads, including one seemingly credible accusation against a man who worked at a uniform supply company. His guilt almost seemed to be confirmed when he fled the city in panic. But as with so many other dead ends, the lead was discounted when the twelfth body turned up by the river on a starry night while the man was under surveillance at his mother's house 200 miles away.

Paul's patience was being tested, and he called me often to talk. There were so many unanswered questions about the motive of this methodical killer, and with little progress, the police thought it wise to once again consult the criminal profiler.

This time the psychological assessment focused on the lack of physical evidence left behind. There was nothing that could be tied to the killer. The doors where he had knocked or on the victims when they were found lacked evidence. The meticulous cleansing of the bodies was particularly telling, the profiler noted, because the killer was going to great lengths to ensure that no clues would be found. The newly refined profile was of a particularly brazen psychopath, feeding on the fear he was causing. He was manipulating the city and taunting police by posing dismembered bodies against a scenic backdrop to show that he was in control of the picture being painted.

And the profiler picked up on something else that was very curious. The absence of fear is a defining personality characteristic of most psychopaths, but the Door Knocker Killer was indeed afraid of something.

He feared losing control.

Control was the predominant theme in the murders, and the profiler believed that the killer would do everything in his power to avoid losing it and getting caught. He was good at manipulating his victims and the public, but he was anxious about the factors that were out of his hands. The killer realized that he had made a mistake when he allowed himself to be captured on video while luring the seventh victim, and the escalation in the cleansing ritual after that was a subconscious effort to maintain control and prevent another misstep that could lead to his capture.

The killer was doing things that ordinary people would find crazy, but he was not insane. In fact, the profiler believed he was depending on logic and reason to plan the crimes, manipulate his victims, and dispose of the bodies cleanly. Someone who relied so heavily on those analytical faculties would not be oblivious to the fact that he had caught a lucky break when shadows obscured his face in the video.

The killer thought he was more intelligent than the investigators, but he recognized that the odds against going undetected forever were nearly impossible. In the back of his mind, he had to be aware that police could surround his house at any moment, and that would raise his anxiety.

A truly rational man who was afraid of losing control would have stopped after being caught on video, Paul thought, but something was compelling the Door Knocker Killer to keep going. He had become addicted to the rush that came with controlling his victims, the public, and police. But he would be keenly aware that he was no longer invisible, and a feeling of impending doom would eat at him. His reasoning was already twisted, and eventually his ability to make logical decisions would degrade as his anxiety gave way to an escalating level of paranoia.

Paul hoped this growing irrationality would cause the killer to make a poor calculation that would lead to his capture before the body count rose further. Or perhaps the man would simply snap under the building pressure and kill himself, choosing to remain in control of his own destiny rather than letting the police and judicial system have the final say. Either way, the murders would stop, and Paul wanted that more than the glory of capturing the Door Knocker Killer.

Not long after Paul and I discussed the new profile report, there was a big break in the case. A local man, a mechanic by trade, walked into police headquarters and said that he wanted to confess.

News trucks ringed City Hall when the mayor proudly announced the arrest. The chief of police thanked all of the officers and detectives who had played a role in bringing the madman to justice, especially Paul. It was a time of self-congratulation and relief, and I noticed a sense of normalcy returning the city.

But the knocking on my door is making me uncomfortable. Ignorance can sometimes be more soothing than knowledge, and while I have found comfort in my pipeline of inside information, I would probably feel more at ease if I didn't know something else.

According to the profile, the type of organized killer who knocks on doors to lure victims into the abyss isn't likely to show up at a police station out of the blue and confess. This might be plausible if he had killed someone close to him, like a family member, and he felt that the police were about to catch him anyway. But investigators can't find a link between the suspect sitting in jail and any of the victims.

A search of the mechanic's apartment and a storage unit he rents turned up many tools, but nothing that can be traced back to the crimes. There were no fibers or fingerprints, and no blood or DNA from the victims. The man didn't even own a bottle of bleach. Most importantly, the police haven't been able to locate the locks of hair and missing body parts that the profiler is certain, the killer is keeping as a collection of souvenirs.

Other detectives think the guy just wanted to dictate of the terms of his own arrest and that there must be a secret lair where everything is hidden, but Paul isn't so sure. Why would a man whose crimes are totally centered around control willingly surrender that for the rest of his life?

I agree with Paul and the profiler that the Door Knocker Killer does not want to be caught. But the question remains: What would possess a man to walk into a police station and confess to crimes he didn't commit? It is curious, I know, but Paul told me that this sometimes happens in high-profile cases. The mechanic might just be one of those attention-starved souls who desperately grabbed for the brightest limelight he could find, consequences be damned.

Paul is on guard against this, though for now, he is enjoying a respite from the pressure. Absent another body showing up, the police are happy to slow-walk the prosecution and let the public believe that all is once again right in the world. But I know too much to find comfort in this.

When I hear the knocking, my imagination gets away from me and takes me to the darkest possible place. Putting aside my fear to open the door for the sake of custom or courtesy could be a costly mistake; the victims certainly learned

127

that lesson the hard way. For all I know, the person on the other side could be in the uniform of a delivery driver, or maybe a policeman, and that thought scares me.

But I can't allow my life to be controlled by fear, and I think that I'll open the door despite my better judgment.

Maybe it's just Paul coming to pay a visit. He often stops by unannounced, and it wouldn't surprise me if he wants to have a drink and talk with someone he can trust. His life is much easier these days without the mayor and chief of police breathing down his neck, but I can tell he's afraid that the real killer isn't sitting in a jail cell downtown. He has a bad feeling that a thirteenth body will soon turn up on display in a park with a lock of hair and some body parts missing. Perhaps that has already happened, and he's coming by to blow off some steam before the pressure drives him mad.

To be perfectly honest, I can't stand Paul. I didn't like him in high school and I don't like him now. And yet, he serves a useful purpose for me. If he's the one knocking on my door, I will happily lend him an ear.

But not one from my collection of souvenirs.

Last Laugh

By John Timm

I could go into great detail about the origins of Clown Day but I'll spare you with a mere summary, handed down to me by an aunt when I was ten. She said it happened when she was a little girl.

The circus train was running late. The engineer failed to slow for Wheeler's Curve just outside town, and the derailment that followed took its toll on man and beast alike, including some thirty clowns who unknowingly gave their final performance in Pittsburgh earlier that evening.

For me, a monument--at most--should have been sufficient. But our town fathers thought otherwise, hoping to turn tragedy into festivity and bring a few dollars into the local coffers in the bargain. On all roads leading into town these days, there's a sign reading, "River Gap, The Clown City, Population 7,148."

***

I don't sleep well. Even worse when I'm preoccupied, which had been my state of mind for weeks, ever since the Clown Day posters went up all around town and our radio station began interviewing the local dignitaries about the coming event as they do every year. While I lay there staring at the ceiling and listening to the trains roll through town one after another, my thoughts flitted from locking myself securely inside, to fleeing elsewhere until all traces of this dreadful ordeal had vanished and calm returned to both our community and my state of mind. My fitful reverie was not to last. Someone began knocking, then pounding, on my door.

"Jamison. Jamison. Open up."

I dressed quickly and headed to the door.

"We need you--and your truck."

"For . . . ?"

"To haul a parade float. Demski's semi broke down. Engines busted. Kelly's Garage worked on it all night. It needs parts from Pittsburgh. They won't be here in time for the parade. Yours is the only other flatbed semi in town big enough to haul the float."

I could have said no. Should have said no. I wanted no part of this clown business. Never in my whole life. But they appealed to my sense of civic duty, and more worn down than willing, I finally gave in. At least I wouldn't be down on the sidewalk with clowns and mimes and a bunch of tourists dressed in weirdo outfits bumping into me, stopping me, making their obnoxious gestures and noises.

***

The parade was set to kick off from the high school at noon. I had to have my truck there by ten so they could move the float from atop Demski's trailer over to mine.

"Thanks, Jamison. We can take care of the rest. Come back maybe around a quarter of twelve so we can be up and running by noon sharp."

There was no sense returning home and having to turn around in less than two hours so I headed over to the Lucky Diner. There's a Clown City Diner here in town too, but I refuse to set foot in it. Whenever I go into the Lucky Diner, they all look at me, then at each other, then down at the floor or out the window or somewhere else. I see it, they think I don't. If there were another place in town, I could get a cup of coffee I'd go there instead—but not the Clown City Diner. No way in hell.

When I returned to the high school, I hardly recognized my truck. They'd draped the sides of the trailer to hide the tires. All you could see of the cab under the decorations were tiny openings over the windshield. The float was nothing more than a high platform with rows of folding chairs. Someone had placed a tall stepladder next to the trailer. *For the dignitaries*, I figured. At five to twelve, I got into the tractor careful not to disturb the decorations. At two minutes to twelve, I saw them coming. Clowns. A whole swarm of ugly, horrible clowns, coming straight towards the truck and me.

"No! Absolutely not. Not on *my* truck."

"Calm down, Jamison. What's the matter with you?"

"I don't want anything to do with clowns. I hate clowns. I've always hated clowns. If you really want to know, they scare me. I'm sure as hell not going to drive a bunch of them around town on my truck." I opened the door and started to get down out of the cab, tearing the decorations.

"Jamison. You've got to help us. I don't get this thing you have about clowns, but we need you to do this."

"I can't," I insisted, as the clowns climbed aboard. By now, my heart was doing double time, the rest of me frozen.

"Jamison, for Pete's sake, just drive the damn truck. Don't look back at the clowns, if that's what bothers you so much."

At once, an indescribable wave came over me. "You're right. I'll drive it." I got back into the cab, they taped over the torn decorations and we edged forward behind the other floats.

***

The parade route was Fifth to Broad. Broad to Main. Left on Main down to Depot. Left again on Depot. I gritted my teeth as we crept along, unable to block out the commotion, the clowns were making an ungodly racket behind me with their bullhorns and laughing, shouting, spraying water and Silly

String. The crowd was egging them on all the while, hooting, whistling, and cheering.

As we approached the corner of Main and Depot, the lights began to flash at the railroad crossing just beyond the intersection. The floats ahead were making the left turn onto Depot Street parallel to the railroad tracks. I could see the Rotary float, the VFW float, the Optimist float. We'd be the next to make the turn. Except we didn't. The gates were down now, the crossing bells were ringing. The train had just rounded Wheeler's Curve. I could hear it picking up speed, sounding its horn. The clowns were still laughing. Laughing hysterically. And so was I, as we drove towards those crossing gates, slowly, breaking through the gates, then stopping, stopping on the tracks, stopping with the trailer behind me, stopping on the tracks, stopping to unhitch the trailer, gunning the tractor forward out of the way, stopping with thirty clowns, thirty clowns laughing, thirty clowns screaming, thirty clowns crying, thirty clowns stopping, stopping on the railroad tracks.

Small Talk

By Paul Griley

They arrived at the cabin at 4:00 in the afternoon, the truck kicking up dust from the dirt parking area alongside the cabin, a brandy bottle and a bag of groceries at her feet in the passenger side. Fifty yards from their front windshield was the river that was surrounded by pine, oak, and birch trees, meandering through the Santa Cruz Mountains on its' way to the ocean. The river splashed along, filling the air with the sound of running water, as if from a fountain left running expressly for them. Simultaneously anxious to see the inside of the rental cabin yet still in the heady days of young love, the two gave each other a quick kiss, got out of the truck and walked toward the cabin.

"This is going to be awesome," he said, smiling at the thought of the weekend ahead of them.

"This place is so cute!" she replied as they got onto the redwood porch in front of the cabin's door.

Inserting the key into the door, he pushed the door open. Inside was a small kitchen with a Formica table and matching counters, alongside a small sitting area with an old plaid couch, a worn armchair, and a throw rug. Behind the front area were two small and sparsely furnished bedrooms, with a small bathroom between the rooms. The cabin was simple, purposefully lacking all the distractions of modern life: no phone, no TV, no radio -- just the two 30-something lovers immersed in the newness of their four-month-old relationship.

Entering the cabin, he looked around the front room and turned to her with a smile.

"Honey, this place is perfect! I'm already on vacation and we just got here," he said.

"There is a little fridge for our food and a coffee maker, they even have dishes and things to cook with," she said as she explored the quaint kitchen area. "I just wish I hadn't forgotten the radio."

"What? Why?"

"In case we run out of things to say," she said, entering the sitting area and noticing the lack of objects to distract the mind.

"Hmm," he said with a shrug, heading out to the truck to get their luggage, groceries, guitars, and ice chest.

After unloading the truck, he lugged in their baggage and chose which of the two bedrooms to use. The two made quick but passionate love, fully appreciating the fact that their cabin was remote, sans neighbors within ear distance.

"That was just a quickie," she said as they put back on their clothes. "There is plenty more where that came from." He turned, grinning, walked to her and gave her a hug.

"You know it, honey," he said, wrapping his arms around her slender waist.

"You got it, baby," she replied with a grunt as he squeezed her waist.

While barbequing hamburgers for dinner, the two talked about their plans for the weekend. They talked about the hiking, the Santa Cruz Boardwalk trip, exploring the town, and the beaches. The conversation continued through dinner. Then came the quick cleanup after dinner, which, included laughs and affection.

After dinner he poured two drinks, brought the cocktails to the couch where she now sat and the two gave each other cheers – *"Cheeries"* – as they clinked their glasses together.

"This was a great idea to come out here, baby," she said, taking a sip of her drink.

"This is going to be a great weekend, honey," he replied, enjoying his own belt from the beverage.

Soon the conversation turned toward whether to go hiking tomorrow or go to the Boardwalk. The two debated the choice for several minutes deciding the boardwalk deserved first dibs. The debate was fun, the choice was easy, and the two contently worked on their cocktails. It was then that he noticed it.

Silence.

In case we run out of things to say echoed through his mind as he recalled the comment. *Shoot, what is she going to think of me if we can't even talk for a few hours? There goes this relationship!!! She's going to think I'm boring!!!* He panicked, slapping his hand on his thigh like a man waging a life and death battle with an invisible fly.

"I've been to three states," he blurted out randomly, raising the pitch on the last two words as if he was asking a question. A spray of the drink she had in her mouth shot out her nose as she coughed. She looked at him confused, her head giving off a slight tic.

Wiping her eyes she said, "Where did that come from? I've been to two states, Florida and New Mexico."

My God! Now what? He couldn't think for himself. He could see inside his own head, but it was like looking at a grey flannel sheet blocking all of his view. He was seeing an imageless void, and then came a floating TV set. *No distractions.* It bobbed through his mind at a bizarre thirty-degree angle, further preventing him from any useful thought. He could feel himself getting warmer, perspiration forming at his temples, hands growing clammy. His sight became fuzzy as he stared at the painting of a river on the wall opposite from the couch.

He noticed there was a fly on the painting. It sat motionless.

Time froze into palpable matter.

After what seemed to him far too long a pregnant pause, she looked at him.

"Well, let's go to bed."

Snapping out of his mind freeze, he thought *saved by the bell.*

The next morning he found himself alone in bed. After a moment of panic that she had left in search of better conversation, he smelled bacon, and simultaneously heard the sound of the bacon crackling in the pan. He looked at the clock. It was 7:30. Rise and shine.

"Good morning, sunshine," she said as he wandered into the kitchen.

"You're up early," he replied, hugging her from behind as she finished preparing breakfast.

"We've got a big day," she said, pulling the bacon out of the frying pan. "You were restless in your sleep last night. You kept squirming."

"Sorry."

Sorry? My, you're a master of conversation!!! A man of many words. He knew he needed to stop fixating on her comment about running out of things to say, but the comment was like a car wreck in his mind, and he couldn't help slowing down to look at it. His thoughts were becoming stuck in a traffic jam.

"Umm, did you sleep okay?" he asked.

"I'm okay. Maybe we can take a nap later," she replied with a grin.

"Yeah," he said.

After breakfast, when they got in the truck to drive to Santa Cruz, he immediately turned on the radio. He encouraged her to find a station to listen to. The coast was about a twenty-minute drive from the cabin. She settled on a talk show focusing on modern day phobias. The hosts were discussing Sedatephobia, which the two were unfamiliar with, but the show came in clear and would kill the time on their drive.

During the drive, they had a brief conversation about the weather and took turns placing their hands on each other's thighs. He was thinking about last night, but he couldn't tell if she even gave the previous night's happenings a second thought.

In Santa Cruz, the two walked along the boardwalk, exploring shops and enjoying some people watching. Conversation flowed easily because there was so much to look at. Around 1:00, they decided they were ready for some lunch and ventured toward the pier, choosing the Fire Fish Grill Restaurant.

After ordering two plates of fish tacos with a calamari appetizer along with a pair of tall beers, the two found and sat at a table in the sun and waited for their food.

"This is so nice out here!" she exclaimed. "I haven't been here in years! It feels so good to get out of the Sacramento heat for a bit. This trip was a great idea! I'm having a great time."

"Me too," he mustered in reply.

"There is such a variety of people here! You have the Rasta hippie kids, the hipster crowd our age, rich people, poor people, but there is such a great vibe! Everyone coexists. This place is so great." She turned to him, love glowing in her eyes. In the distance, a sea otter was loudly exclaiming its own love of the area.

"I know. It's great." *Car wreck, slow down, gotta look, can't...help...it!* He was getting flustered again.

"Are you okay?" she asked. "You look pale. You don't look well."

"I'm alright," he replied. "I just need to stand up and move for a bit."

With that, he got up and walked out onto the wharf.

When the food arrived, he returned to the table and the two greedily began devouring the calamari. Apparently, they were hungrier than they thought and the food was indeed delicious.

After lunch and a brief walk, they decided to return to the cabin to rest a bit and see what the evening would bring.

At the cabin, they made love again and soon thereafter fell asleep.

He woke up alone again. Glancing at the clock, he noticed it was almost 4:00. A good little nap. Getting out of bed, he realized how quiet the cabin was. Not a sound. Emptiness.

He found her sitting on the couch in the front room. She was looking out the window.

"I miss having a TV," she stated as she noticed him entering the room.

"We've made it a day now, honey," he offered in reply.

"I know, but I just want to relax. I don't want to talk. I don't want to think," she said.

He looked at her and nodded. Sitting next to her, putting his arm around her shoulder, he could not believe his luck.

Irrational Fears

The Prettiest Mama

By Robin Becker

I'm finally meeting Jason, my future husband, in the flesh today. We hooked up online weeks ago on a herpes-dating site—matches for 25% of the population, the banner ad says. I registered for the site even though I don't have herpes. I call my affliction *virtual herpes* because if things work out with Jason, or anyone else I might meet, I plan to contract the eternal H the first time we express our love physically. That way, he'll never know I didn't have sores before. It's a romantic gesture, this secret love gift, a forever-genital bond I am covertly allowing him to share with me.

My relationship with Jason is already intimate. In other words, we've had sex. Cybersex, of course. Dirty typing. His throbbing meat, my love canal, his rod, my honey pot, his love tool, my little cunnie, his passion pole, my creamy crevice, his manhood, my whatever. I typed with both hands on the keyboard for fear of sullying my ergonomically designed computer chair with my love juice. Judging from his typos, my future husband wasn't too concerned about his chair.

We're rendezvousing at Jazzland, a theme park located twenty minutes outside of New Orleans. It was Jason's idea. He loves theme parks. I hate them for one simple reason: I'm afraid of throw up. Deathly afraid of throw up. Heart-pounding, sweaty-palm-screaming, run-for-your-life afraid of throw up. On a roller coaster, there's an increased chance that someone, probably some carrot-top brat who's eaten too many funnel cakes and soft-serve ice cream, will puke and some of it might get on me. Even smelling the stuff sets me off and I can't hear a cough in the next toilet stall without pulling up my panties, mid-stream if necessary, and bolting.

When Jason and I made our plans on the phone, I didn't mention these worries. My Daddy taught me a girl should show interest in a man's interest, even if she's not interested. Then again, Mama up and left Daddy and me one day years ago and we never did figure out why.

I arrived at Jazzland early. I want to eat a Jazzburger and drink a strawberry daiquiri alone. Eating calms me, and more importantly, I won't have to eat with Jason later. He'd think it was gross, the way I chew and swallow, and particularly the noises I make in the back of my throat. Daddy says Mama made those same noises and that men find them earthy and attractive, but here I disagree with him. To me they sound like the satisfied grunts of a welfare mother eating pork rinds and drinking orange coke while watching Court TV on the day bed.

After lunch, I find a restroom and the first thing I do is the first thing I always do in public bathrooms: kick open empty stall doors searching for stray throw up. A few women look at me askance, but I ignore them and reapply my lipstick— Amethyst Gold by Mac—in the warped plastic mirror. I smooth my shorts, which make me look slimmer than I am, although I am by no means fat. I am a woman who carries her weight well. All 152.5 pounds of me are distributed in a pleasing, curvy manner, a figure my daddy calls hourglass. What's more, the womanly flesh is lying smooth as meringue, not wrinkling into the unsightly curdles, bumps, and ridges you see on so many poor girls. Even thin ones.

I saunter out of the bathroom and enter Jazz Plaza, a magical place filled with quaint shops selling alligator-claw back-scratchers and plastic crawfish. I spot Jason right off. He's standing in front of the Basin Street Bakery, checking his watch. He looks exactly like his profile pic: khaki chinos, button-down blue oxford, and very tall, over six feet, but with a bit of a belly jutting out. He reminds me of a big Teddy Bear with that cuddly belly. And he still has all his hair even though he's 38. Thank God for that. I walk up to him.

"You must be Jason," I say. "I'm Amber. Amber Fontenot."

I stick out my hand in a formal way, drooping the fingers a little so it becomes his choice whether to clasp the entire hand professionally and firmly or touch the fingers in a gentlemanly fashion as if my hand were something delicate and sacred and he has nothing to prove with a firm handshake. Happily, he chooses the latter.

"Nice to meet you in person," he says.

He's staring at my tits, which is good. I didn't wear this plunging, plum-colored Gap t-shirt for him to look at my hair, which I nevertheless had cut and colored yesterday for this exact moment. I smile broadly at him.

"Here we are," he says.

I stick my chin out and nod.

"Are you hungry?" he asks.

"I had a salad right before I left Baton Rouge, so I'm set for a while."

"Did you say you've never been here before?"

I nod again. "This is my first time."

"Wanna walk around?" he asks. "Maybe hit some rides?"

"Absolutely!"

I scan the area for kids who appear nauseous or as though they might become nauseous after eating a Jazzburger and torturing their bodies with unnatural upside-down and side-to-side motions, not to mention sheer, terrifying drops of 100 feet or more. No one is holding their stomach and no one is leaning over a garbage can. On the other hand, everyone is a potential puker.

Emetophobia. The Latin name alone proves it's a documented, researched fear like claustrophobia or carcinophobia. My best friend Tiffany claims the only way to conquer fear is to confront it head on, and to that end she offered, back in her bulimic days, to throw up into a bucket in front of me. It was her belief that once I realized nothing bad would happen, the fear would disappear and I'd be free. She's a good friend, but I had to decline.

"Amber?" Jason asks. "Are you okay? You've gone white as a sheet."

I put my hand on my cheek, which feels hot as pavement. "Just a little peaked all of a sudden."

Jason steers me around the fountain at the park's entrance and towards Cajun Country. We walk through a village filled with artisans selling silver jewelry, stained glass, and pottery.

"You know what I love about theme parks?" Jason asks.

Since I don't think an answer is required, a brief pause ensues.

"The way they imitate real life," he continues. "Like here in Louisiana, we have Cajun Country. What am I saying? We *are* Cajun Country. But it's replicated at Jazzland, only better, because of the rides. We can also go to Mardi Gras every day here and not worry about getting mugged or beaten up. It's totally safe. Of course we won't see any tits." Jason leers at me. "Or will we?"

Someone is going to throw up on me. I can feel it. It might even be Jason.

"They've got the old-timey Pontchartrain Beach Boardwalk here, too," he says. "The original Pontchartrain Beach closed in the early 80s. You're probably too young to have gone there or if you did you wouldn't remember. It was cool, but I bet the Jazzland version is even cooler. Have you been to Busch Gardens in Virginia? They've got it divided up into six different European countries. The best ride there is the Alpengeist. It's in Switzerland, I think."

Two screaming kids run past ambushing us from behind, pushing on my hips and butt as they barrel toward the Muskrat Scrambler, a ride that resembles the children's game Mousetrap.

"Calm down!" the kids' mother yells. She's a middle-aged woman wearing stiletto heels with yellow camel-toe Capris. She totters after her children wobbling on those shoes.

"Have you been to Switzerland?" I ask Jason. Frankly, I don't care if he has or not, but I must distract him because we're standing at the entrance to the Muskrat Scrambler now. Jason hesitates. He wants to ride it.

"Just the one at Busch Gardens." He holds out his hand. "This ride's a classic. It's usually called the Wild Mouse, but I've been on the Psycho Mouse, the Mad Mouse, and the Crazy Mouse. They're all the same basic design though."

I'm on the threshold of a hairpin-turn ride named after a rodent; I'm about to push through the turnstile and pull down the safety harness. This is the moment when I should give up and tell him everything: I'm sorry, Jason, but I hate roller coasters, I'm afraid of vomit, I don't have herpes, my mother left me, and I faked my online orgasms. A true gentleman would understand.

"They should call it the Nutty Nutria Rat," I say, putting my hand in his.

Jason laughs. "C'mon, Amber. Let's ride it!"

In the fifth grade, I entered a beauty contest called Little Miss Cotton. I wore a fluffy white communion-style dress and pink ballet slippers, but I lost to Kristie Thibodeaux, who wore a slinky black evening gown and shoes with miniature heels. Daddy said she looked like a grown-up slut while I looked like an angel. Regardless, she's the one who wore the crown.

"What's the best ride here?" I ask, staring up at Jason's chin, which is not quite as strong and angular as the chins of the Fontenot men, but it's not face pudding either. For him, I will be like Kristie Thibodeaux—brave and utterly not myself.

"The MegaZeph," he says.

"Tell me about it."

"It's in the Mardi Gras section of the park. It's homage to the Zephyr, which used to be at Pontchartrain Beach, so I don't know why they put it in Mardi Gras. That's not in keeping with history. The coaster's structure is wooden, not steel..."

"The drops!" I yell. "The dips and the drops. I need to know about thrills, not construction material!"

"Are you okay?" Jason asks for the second time.

"Thirsty," I croak.

We walk to a stand where Jason buys me a lemonade served in a plastic lemon with a Crazy Straw sticking out of the top. I finish in one breath, not even offering Jason a sip, and tuck the souvenir lemon into my purse.

"I'm ready for the MegaZeph," I announce.

To reach Mardi Gras, we have to walk through Pontchartrain Beach, which really is set up like an old-time boardwalk complete with a small strip of sand that is, unfortunately, inaccessible to the public. There's a guess your weight and age booth (what woman would subject herself to that in public?), in addition to games of chance and skill, including my favorite, the one where you shoot a stream of water into the clown's mouth.

"Let me try and win you something," Jason says, heading for the basketball hoops. His choice of games is either rudely symbolic or utterly thoughtless and inconsiderate. If he were successful, the prize would be Miss Piggy in a tutu.

"I'd really like to hit that coaster," I say, grabbing Jason by the elbow and pulling him away from the plethora of Miss Piggys, all of whom are mocking me with that "I'm fat and sexy" attitude she manages to pull off. The porker.

"An eager little beaver!" Jason says, gazing down at me as we walk.

I ignore him, although I can't help but remember he used that exact phrase during one of our chats. He has rosy cheeks and they're glowing as if he's smeared on cheap rouge. His teeth are straight and clean.

We get in line behind a Baptist youth group decked out in bright orange T-shirts complete with tacky black crosses splashed across their backs.

"I'm really glad you're Catholic," I tell Jason.

"Not practicing," he says.

"That doesn't matter. My Daddy says it's like being Jewish. If you're born a Catholic, you die a Catholic. Where'd you take your First Communion?"

"Our Lady Queen of Peace. It's in Baltimore."

"I love that you're not from here. It makes you different. Exotic."

The Baptist youth group ahead of us fills up the roller coaster.

"We're next, Amber. You excited?"

"Thrilled."

Another train pulls up, and Jason races through the turnstile.

"Let's ride in the front car!" he says.

I inspect the area. No one appears pale, green, or even tired. Every face is happy with anticipation, as if everyone is posing for the Jazzland brochure. There is no dread here, I realize. When something is this carefully planned, dread is not an option.

Jason pulls down the harness bar for me and puts his hand on my knee. The pimply-faced attendant checks the bar for security then we chug up the incline. The coaster makes that cranky, clanking noise, creaking like the chain might break.

The first drop is 110 feet, 65 miles per hour, and there's no windshield. There is laughter like crying and screams like burning witches. The wind is in my hair like a TV commercial. This ride's the Declaration of Independence and the Magna Carta! The Spirit of '76 and the Rebel Flag! I momentarily forget that I don't have herpes and that vomit equals death. Jason throws his hands up in the air and I imitate him. I imagine bugs are flying into my mouth, and I imagine they taste like crawfish.

During the third dip, when my stomach drops dangerously close to my knees and my neck aches from the whips and turns, I recall the talk I had with Mama the night she ran away from home. I was five and she was my exact age now, twenty-five.

"Amber," she told me, "you won't understand this right away…"

She was so beautiful, her big blonde hair encircling her face like an Eskimo's parka, her lipstick that Daddy called Draconian Red, and her perfume like raw sugar cane. When she bent close to me, I smelled whiskey and coke.

She smoothed back my hair and her bracelets made music.

"Amber," she said, "you won't understand this now, but I can't go horseback riding with you tomorrow."

"Why not?"

She patted her curls into place. But they were never out of place.

"You're the prettiest, Mama."

That made her laugh. "What if I don't care to be the prettiest Mama anymore?"

"You have to come horseback riding!"

"I can't. But I suspect your Daddy will get along just fine without me. And so will you. I promise."

She kissed me then leaving a mark on my cheek in the shape of her lips, a mark I refused to wash off until Daddy made me, arguing that I couldn't attend Mass if I was dirty. It's a mark I still see in my imagination whenever I apply my blush (Clinique's Coral Pink) in the mirror.

"Amber!" Jason is waving his hand in front of my face. "Are you okay?"

The ride's over. I inhale deeply, sniffing for vomit.

"I'm a little shaky," I reply.

Jason lends me his elbow as we exit the train. My knees are wobbly and my neck is tense. A few feet away from the MegaZeph we see a Mardi Gras parade rolling by. Automatically I lift up my hands and catch a string of purple beads. They're cheap, the kind only little kids and tourists wear, but instead of throwing them back like I would during a real parade, and I unsnap the flimsy latch and put them around my neck.

"Pretty," Jason says.

"You think so?" I finger the beads like a rosary. Hail Mary, full of grace. Blessed art thou among women.

Jason rests his hand on my shoulder, squeezing it as he guides me away from the parade. We walk by a bench, and sure enough, there's a carrot-top kid sitting on it with his head between his knees. His mama's rubbing his back and smoothing his hair. I slow my pace and meet her eyes.

"The MegaZeph," she explains. Her son's skinny body starts to convulse.

I walk to the other side of the boy and put my hand on top of his head like I'm blessing him. I feel confident, ready to confront whatever he might spew. He opens his mouth and out it streams—chunky, gooey, hot, and yellow. Right onto the sidewalk. A smidgen splatters my Kenneth Cole sandal and grazes my big toe. Nothing bad happens.

"Poor little fella," I comfort him. "Let it out. Let it all out."

"He rode that contraption three times in a row," his mother says. "I warned him."

The boy wretches again. I move my hand to the back of his wiry neck. This gesture is important. What I say next should reflect my wisdom and reinforce for Jason how effortlessly maternal I'm being, what a good mother I'll make. How I'll never leave.

"He'll learn soon enough," I say. "You best listen to your mama."

"Now I'm starting to feel sick." Jason puts his hand over his paunch.

The mother and I look at each other and some knowledge passes between us, old as Genesis.

"You better go," she says. "We don't want both our boys sick."

Jason takes off for Pontchartrain Beach at an almost-run, while I promenade behind him like it's Easter Sunday and I'm wearing a brand new outfit. I find him in front of Mad Rex, a whirling, spinning, vomit-wheel of a ride.

"Are you okay?" I ask.

"That smell," he says. "It always makes me queasy."

Jason's cheeks have turned from rosy red to a curious combination of lime and olive. He's panting like a dog. I start walking away from Mad Rex and he follows me.

"Where are you going?" he asks.

"I want to ride the merry-go-round." I turn to face him. "The horses."

"You mean Mardi Gras Menagerie," he says, swallowing hard. "It's not in Pontchartrain Beach. It's back in Mardi Gras."

He needs to sit down, poor dear. I take his hand and lead him to a bench.

"Let me warn you," he says, lowering his head between his knees. "Mardi Gras Menagerie doesn't have just horses like you'd expect. True to its name, it's a menagerie. It's got camels, rabbits, frogs, you name it. I don't want you to be disappointed."

This future husband of mine, this fan of theme park trivia, lover of rides and roller coasters, and this sick and lonely man—he's worrying about my happiness.

But Mama was right; I'll be fine.

I lay my head on his back as he begins to heave. I close my blue-powdered eyes and I am not afraid. On the contrary, I look forward to mounting my carousel horse.

SILENT NIGHT

By Thomas Elson

"**Y**ou're kidding. Anderson's seeing a patient on Christmas Eve?" the physician said to his colleague standing in the quiet hospital corridor. Both men unable to keep their eyes off the patient - her tailored pantsuit, strands of layered hair falling past her shoulders. However, it was her eyes they remembered—piercing green eyes, seared by red tributaries.

"Yep, every year around this time, that tall redhead, Dr. Renée Maxwell, makes the same request. Something about her father." He looked at his colleague, "Have you seen her office? Looks like a damn shrine to the guy." They watched as Anderson ushered his patient into the office and left the door ajar.

***

Years earlier, on a thawed, sunny morning, two days before Christmas, in a time before computers and instant searches, Kevin Maxwell repeated his morning routine. First, he fed his cat, left water and food for her inside the garage, and then poured water in her preferred sidewalk divot. He noticed the flashing lights across the street through Mrs. Reynolds' picture window and watched as her Irish setter returned from his solo morning walk.

Fourteen years to get to this point and proud of where those years had brought him - a five-bedroom house, his second wife was no longer the bunion in his life because he divorced and deposited her sixteen miles away teaching with the graduate degree Kevin financed. He was now a single man with a house and a good income in an area not known for either.

He had joint custody of his daughter, Renée. He could hear his mother's voice, "when you're with Renée, you take on an aura and walk taller." He reveled in his little girl's pride and respect. However, he lived in fear of exposure. If anyone knew, if exposed, he would rather die than face his daughter.

During his unvarying daily, commute from house to office, traveling through a town frozen in the nineteenth century where people were clinging to fables from the cattle era. He drove past the red and white three-story Renaissance Courthouse with the Sheriff's office on the third floor then turned near the limestone tower of the Ninnescah State Bank, which has been on that same corner since 1878. The bank's atmosphere has been fractured since state agents – based upon allegations molded into evidence by ambitious prosecutors - removed the bank owner and his family.

He veered into his reserved parking spot and entered his office by a private door. Once seated, he unlocked his credenza, looked inside, relaxed, leaned against his leather chair, and then pulled it slowly toward his newly refinished oak desk. He then glanced at his desk calendar, stretched, walked through the front offices adorned with paintings from local artists, then angled toward the stairwell.

He made his way up the stairway framed with the awards and letters he has received from elected officials and the copies of front-page coverage for development projects obtained for cities and counties- Kevin's picture was everywhere. Lines written by women reporters: "His Lincolnesque figure dominated the meeting." Another wrote, "Tall, articulate, lauded by Mayors and City Managers for his guiding hand and skill." He turned left at the landing and greeted the second floor staff members as they prepared project drafts for his review.

* * *

A lifetime ago, on a Sunday evening, Sherry Maxwell, a woman Renée would never know, lay abandoned inside a shed underneath the floorboards. She had never been so cold.

Thirty miles to the East, her husband, Kevin Maxwell, who, in a few years, would be Renée's father, was also cold. Late night, limestone in winter, temperature below 30, wind above 40, cold.

Earlier that night, alone inside her car, Sherry heard a crunching sound. As she looked out, a gloved hand pulled the

160

door open. The other hand reached for her left shoulder. The man glared at her. "Well? Tell me." His hand hit the steering wheel. His normally calm voice was gone. "Tell me now."

Sherry tried to swallow. Her throat was too dry. She coughed. In a flash, she was on the passenger side. *Not again.* Behind the wheel, he shifted gears, drove over the icy surface road until he reached the comparatively dry I-70 entrance ramp – headed west.

During their dinner that evening, Sherry had been full of recriminations. *She told me about the camping trip with her vague friend, and then started in on me.* "You should have done..." "You should have been ..." "Why didn't you..." and her default position, "If only you had, then..." Followed by the inevitable, "I have decided ..."

Inside his car, Kevin looked at the slanted falling white flakes, soon to become black ice and then brown slush. Ice clung to his windshield. With his right hand, he shoved the heater lever far into the red. He shoved it repeatedly until he heard it click. With his left hand, he pulled his coat collar higher, grabbed the steering wheel and drove away, alert against the cold vinyl seat as if eager to receive guidance.

Images of Sherry emerged. The tall, leggy young woman in short skirts, movements like a breeze. That night, Kevin's body felt the same initial electrical charge. *Nobody else's. Mine.*

She was, as her father said, "a sleek-moving sports car on the country road of life."

East on I-70, he slowed and flipped an almost legal U-turn, circled back west to Brookvale past the snow-covered parking lot in front of the darkened restaurant. *Just a quick look – just to see.* Her car was where he had parked it. Farther west – he stopped at the shed enclosed within a grove of trees. Inside that shed, beneath the floorboards a few feet underground, nothing had been disturbed. Drove away relieved. He needed to go back to their house and re-pack for Jeffersonville.

Before he left town, Kevin called Sherry. He knew she would not be at home, but he had always called on his way out of town. Her phone rang. He left a message. Then he placed a second call to Sherry's new employer. "Sherry asked me to call. We're moving out-of-state, she won't be able to take the job after all."

Kevin passed Agnes City, whose residents were either on their way up, on their way down, or on their way out. *Sherry said if I got steady work, she'd marry me. Her second marriage. I got the work. When that work took me out-of-state, she wouldn't move with me.*

Six months earlier, Kevin had come home to an empty house. *She started staying out late. When at home, she'd answer my questions with one-syllable answers. I got tired of hearing, 'fine', 'good', 'okay', 'yes', 'no'. Sometimes when I'd answer the phone, the caller would hang up. Then she'd 'should' all over me.* "You shoulda been better, shoulda been faster, longer, shoulda been more, more," Kevin whispered.

Kevin retreated to the early years of his marriage. *Her parents didn't like me. Never really got any acceptance from them. All the years they we were married, they never invited us to Christmas dinner. But she and I seemed okay.* Kevin saw his breath and felt the wind sway his car.

An eighteen-wheeler passed abruptly swerving into Kevin's lane. He turned the steering wheel to the right with the gentle motion of someone practiced in winter driving. *Could have gone over the embankment. That driver wouldn't even feel the hit. Just driven away.* Stopped, caught his breath. Looked in the back. Exhaled. Drove on.

Skirted the Prairie Parkway - never cut, never pastured. On through the embittered Verdigris County where conspiracy and paranoia had always been rife, its' mirror images reflected in sparse landscape and inhabitants. Hunched shoulders, stooped backs, clenched fists, and universal gun racks corroborated their belief that some omnipresent force planned to take something from them, unless they remained alert and fully armed.

***

Kevin bypassed Jeffersonville, fought snow and ice for hours afterward. Now, inside a motel room, shoved the thermostat past 75, tossed his duffel bag on the edge of the bed, washed his hands several times. Pulled back the thick, dull, plastic curtains, glared out the picture window, his eyes followed the falling snow. Felt the wind inside the motel room. He searched for his wife's logic.

Married to me, she planned to spend the next two days with some other guy. Camping. Wouldn't tell me who. Says she's afraid of my temper. Probably right. Tonight, when I saw her, I, well, no point in thinking about that. Kevin jerked the shades shut, flipped a finger toward the ceiling, drifted toward the bed, and worried.

***

Fourteen years later, on Christmas Eve, Kevin walked into his office, heard his name called by a man swaddled in a dark blue suit, tie, socks, shoes, personality. He had talked with this same man two years earlier during the Ninnescah State Bank investigation. He had hoped the man would never come back.

The agent threw a series of questions at him. Then, just as the last time, delivered a caveat, saying, "I'll be in touch."

Kevin, stunned, sat and watched as the agent walked out the private entrance and drove toward the sheriff's offices.

Warrants, fueled by political bias, would soon carpet the county. Had he asked, he could have fought it – maybe come back better than before. But he didn't. He knew his life would be ripped open.

His secretary stepped into his office and asked about the meeting. "Can't say. Can only tell you I was told not to talk." He looked at her, "I'll be back in an hour." Before he left, he pulled a box from his credenza.

***

Before he left town, Kevin ran errands. First - his daughter's recital dress and high-heeled tap-shoes placed the boxes in the trunk. She wanted to quit dance lessons last year, but he insisted on one more year – her year to dance in heels. He knew with her height, any solo attempts to wear heels would be coupled with a slump, followed by back problems.

The next stop was David's Discount where, last summer, Kevin bought his daughter's .22 training pistol. He had promised to teach her how to fire a shotgun this summer. Walked directly to the gun shop. Within minutes, the salesman placed a shotgun and shells in a box, which also went into the trunk of the car.

At his ex-wife's apartment, Kevin inserted the key she insisted he keep – so she would not be inconvenienced when he returned with Renée from their time together. Carried boxes into the kitchen, placed them on the kitchen counter, finished a

165

note to Renée. On his way out, he placed one of the boxes in the corner of his daughter's closet. Walked through the living room, left for McDonald's. Ordered a cheeseburger, exited the drive-thru, headed west.

***

Twelve hours after the state agent walked out of his office, Kevin Maxwell turned onto a familiar, isolated county road. Then he made an immediate right onto a more isolated road. As the sunset faded into a starless, silent night, the interior of his car echoed the quiet. He noticed his McDonald's bag was unopened.

A quick dogleg barely wide enough for his car, then, just as before, camouflaged inside a grove of trees – the familiar shed. Pulled the car behind the shed. Removed one box from the trunk.

He knew once inside the shed it would take weeks, years, if ever. Opened the door, did a practiced scan. The weathered walls sagged. Pressed his hand against the wall, felt it give. Noticed the straw behind the familiar cylinder that, years earlier, had reminded him of a root beer barrel. He sat on it. Glanced at the floorboards. Discharged rapid-fire Acts of Contrition. Nothing had changed. Multiple thoughts and emotions – all funneled into one decision.

Irrational Fears

On that silent Christmas Eve, had he asked, he might have made a different decision. Had he asked, his redheaded daughter would not be telling her story in a psychiatric hospital on Christmas Eve. Had he asked, those frail walls would not have shattered from the impact of his skull fragments.

Unravelled

By Casey Douglass

Screeching machinery wailed at Mark's back as he entered the dirt smeared beer tent, the thick material doing little to smother the noise once he was inside. He coughed as the odours of alcohol, tobacco, and body odour tickled the back of his throat. He glanced around the surprisingly empty tent, the only denizens were his cluster of giggling university friends playing drinking games in the far corner. A face crested above the gaggle of heads and locked eyes with his.

'Mark! Over 'ere mate! What kept ya? Ya knew the rides stop early tonight!'

Mark shrugged and crossed the cigarette-strewn floor, wary of standing in the areas that looked like they might be sticky. The conversation petered out as he sat at the end of the table, broken matchsticks and peanuts littering the battle-worn surface like salty casualties of war.

'Evening,' he said, trying to give his most genuine looking smile. His insides churned as the crew looked at him, the people who by default had become his friends. They all had the same class schedule, lived in the same university housing, and even ate in the same places. It was as if a magnetic force had pushed them all together. Mark pondered if the magnetic force had any sense whatsoever. They weren't his kind of people but he forced himself to be sociable. It was better than the alternative.

'Well?' William said.

'Well what?' Mark smiled harder and returned William's stare.

'I asked what kept ya?'

'Oh yes! I had to finish a report that's due tomorrow.'

'Really?'

'Yes.'

'You weren't spinning around for hours?' William's face scrunched into a smirk.

The others tittered; one of the girls, Michelle, snorted into her Rum and Coke.

Mark felt his body go south. It wasn't a literal thing, just the feeling of his stomach slipping into one leg, his heart into the other, thumping and palpitating all the way down. The smile was the only thing that stayed put. 'Really.'

'Ah I'm only joshin' with ya, come up ta the bar with me and I'll buy ya a pint. Ya see that barmaid looking as ya came in? Think she'd spread'em nice an' wide for ya mate!'

Mark looked across at the barmaid, William's voice still hanging in the air. She looked away, her cheeks burning crimson.

'Classy Will!' Michelle hissed.

'It's bloody true! Come on Marky!' William slapped the table and stood, his lopsided swaying carrying him away like a freshly unleashed spinning top.

Mark pushed himself up and caught up in a few long strides, his mind wondering what the poor girl would say. He risked a glance in her direction but she was looking away towards the tent entrance. He walked into the back of the now stationary William, knocking his chin on his right shoulder.

'Why did you-,'

'A dance!' William yelled. He grabbed Mark's hands and began to turn him, spinning Mark around and around until Mark's shoes bit into the dirt floor and brought everything to an abrupt halt. William wheeled away and crashed against the bar, his backside half on a barstool. His face was red, his mouth locked in a Cheshire grin.

Mark felt sick. The room was still spinning around him even though he'd come to a standstill. His heart hammered, his fists clenched, a feeling of tightness seared around his midriff. He yelled and began to spin in the opposite direction, his lips mouthing the count as he tried to estimate the rotations needed.

'One...two...three...'

He realized he was spinning too quickly and reversed direction again, trying to equalize the ripping tingling in his abdomen. He panted, his face glistening with perspiration. Yes, there, no there!

'Minus one...zero...one...'

He adjusted and re-adjusted until it all felt right. He sucked in a labored breath and blew it out through his teeth, his ears a hiss of static and blood pressure...and laughter.

He looked back at his so-called friends, one of the girls with her hand between her legs shouting about how she'd almost pissed herself, the boys punching the air and hooting. Mark looked at the pretty barmaid. She had a hand to her mouth, her whole body shaking with the effort of suppression, wet tears running down the back of her hand. She snorted. Mark ran from the tent, the fiery acid of shame burning through his veins.

Mark walked for some time, the moments not measured in seconds but the creeping garishness of the fairground at night. Rides whizzed and whirled on all sides, people screamed and laughed. Couples passed, hand in hand, oblivious to all around them save for the eyes of their lover, their soul mate, their fuck buddy. Mark felt a heavy stone pushing down in his stomach. Stall owners barked their wares: games, novelties and cheap teddy bears that looked like they'd been sat on by some obese roadster before being pinned on display by their ears. It all washed past Mark, his only concern was avoiding the milling crowds and not getting in the way. He snorted. It was the story of his life.

His cheeks still burned but the evening breeze rolling in from the sea cooled them a little. A clown bounced past, his white face-paint cracked and gaping, his tobacco- stained teeth locked in an ivory grin as he parped his horn in Mark's ear. He dashed away, a syrupy chuckle receding into the crowd. Mark's eyes began to prickle as he found a dark wooden bench at the edge of the fair and fell exhausted and trembling onto its graphited surface.

'Just another freak at the fair!' he hissed.

He hadn't asked for this fucking thing, this obsession with rotation. He certainly hadn't revealed it to anyone around him, not intentionally anyway, they just picked up on it. Well, they'd have to be blind not to.

He couldn't remember when it started, but he had memories of it from a young age. It might have started as a game, some idle distraction of a creative child bored at having nothing to challenge him mentally as he grew. He remembered getting out of the car after a shopping trip with his mum, walking behind her and being asked to get the last bag from the back seat. He remembered turning, opening the car door, lifting the bag, closing the door, and then having this feeling of a length of string wrapped around his midriff. He did what anyone might do if they didn't stop to question it and rotated in the opposite direction when he'd opened the door. The string feeling went away and life moved on. Until it came back! That feeling happened again and again, the sense of a piece of string, changing to rope, to wire and now to barbed wire. That almost tingling mental impression of something coiling around him now felt like a constricting force that was trying to squeeze his insides out through his mouth! He trembled as he ruminated, the same origin story running through his mind over and over yet offering no more wisdom on the thousandth time than the first. He guessed it was an anxiety thing, that he just needed to live with it and not give in and it would go away. It was easy to think like that when not in its grip though. When he was having 'an attack', he thought he was going to die. He intended to see someone, a counsellor or therapist, it just never materialized, they either fobbed him off or he was too busy with university and his shitty shop job. Who has the time to be sane?

'There you are!' a dark figure cried as it emerged from the last of the stalls.

Mark strained his eyes to see who it was, the voice familiar. As the person neared, he saw the pockmarked weasel face of Colin, the runt who followed William around like a pet poodle.

'What do you want Colin?'

'We were worried!'

'Bullshit!'

'Really! William wants to make it up to you; he didn't think you'd go batshit on us!'

'William can get fucked! You all can!'

Colin stood over him and shrugged. 'He got that barmaid's number for you...'

Mark tried to keep an impassive expression but felt a grin escape the prison of his lips. 'Really?'

Colin nodded. 'Saw him myself! She felt sorry for you I think, after she stopped laughing!'

Mark felt his stomach jump a loop the loop. He was wary of what William might be up to, but surely another prank wouldn't be baited with an insult in the message. Mark's mind pulled him this way and that. It warned him at first but then gave him the go-ahead. He didn't know many girls, let alone date them. 'Alright then.'

'That's the spirit! I told him the prospect of a bit of action would get you back!'

Mark smiled and stood, his thoughts mulling over the minimal chances of Colin ever suggesting anything to William.

Mark didn't react to the hands grabbing his arms and legs until it was far too late. He yelled at the top of his lungs but the crowd around him thought it was just some drunken game. He lashed out with his right foot but it failed to come free from the iron grip around his ankle.

'Steady there mate!' William said as he loomed into Mark's view. 'Don't want ta mess up the surprise!'

'What surprise!' Mark shrilled.

The group laughed, William the loudest. 'The surprise! *The* surprise! The one that'll cure ya once and for all!'

'Cure me?'

'Of ya spinny thing!'

Through the tangle of bodies and limbs, Mark spied a ride getting nearer and nearer. A big bulb-lit sign proclaimed it as "The Tilt-A-Whirl". He screamed.

He screamed as they shouted to the operator that he was the one. He screamed as he watched money grease oil-caked palms. He screamed as they put him in one of the cars and locked his wrists in place with pink fluffy handcuffs. He screamed and screamed. The high-pitched wheeze from his lungs mingling with the rattling motor as the ride lurched into its well-worn circular motion. He heard his laughing abductors jumping away with whoops and shouts as his head began to loll to one side. The car began to spin faster and faster, everything mashing into streams of neon light and whirring noises. He squeezed his eyes shut but that failed to relieve any of the sensations that assailed his body. He felt like a lone mind orbiting the event horizon of a black hole, the pressure sucking at his insides as he neared the crushing singularity. He sobbed as through the dizziness and nausea, another feeling began to emerge. Sharp barbs began to rip into his stomach, rending flesh and tearing muscle. His hands gripped the bar in front of him as pain flowed up his body, knuckles white, jaw clenched. Everything began to hiss, to grow faint, the noise, the spinning feeling, like it was all happening at a great distance.

When he woke, the handcuffs were gone, the music had stopped and all about him was still and quiet. A rattling came from somewhere off to his left. He spied the ride operator arms deep in an open hatchway. Mark struggled to stand, his shaking legs driving his shoes onwards, sidestepping the puke that had pooled in the foot-well. 'Hey! I want to ride again!' he squeaked.

'Huh?' the baseball capped man expelled as he squinted at Mark.

'The ride!' Mark wheezed. His insides tight and bubbling as the pressure pressed in on his abdomen. 'I need to ride again, but going around the other way!'

'Fuck off! You and your mates already caused me enough grief tonight. It ain't enough I've got to wipe up your sick; the sodding ride is shot to buggery. Go faster they fucking said. I should have known it wouldn't hold up to that!'

'It's not working?' Mark wailed.

'Fucking Sherlock!' the man said before turning back to his work.

Mark screeched and ran, a mad beast dancing among the dark skeletons of candy-floss stalls and dodgems, the light and movement that once energized them withdrawn and gone leaving their shadowy corpses for the seagulls to shit on. Stragglers jumped out of his way as he careened through them, the wide-eyed pale banshee breaking their own revelries, showing them that even if they were having fun, not all was well with the world. He left the boundary of the fairground and ran on the beach, the twinkling lights of the harbor down the coast beckoning and cold.

Exhaustion overtook him and he fell to the sand clutching his belly, his sides threatening to split and spill his innards across the soft footprint indented surface. He grimaced and lay on his back, letting off another wail at the dull clouds that masked the stars. He stared up into smeary blackness, the cooling breeze now goose-bump inducing and chilly. His mind was empty, his body full of pain.

Slowly...painstakingly... he started to roll.

THE END

Klepto

By Erin O'Loughlin

*C*rossing Ebisubashi Bridge in the heart of downtown Osaka, I pass the Glico chocolate sign, its RGB palette pulsing in time with my tell-tale heart. In the corner of my eye, the Glico man impossibly turns his head and winks at me from his neon chapel. I shiver and hurry across the bridge. Osaka's beloved symbol, like me, is an oversized alien in this land of slight people.

Six-foot and strawberry-blond, I am a picture that's been photocopied at +10%. I tower over the people on the bridge, pushing through the dark-haired crowds. They are all meeting friends or lovers, or looking for new ones, here under the gaze of the Glico man who is running across his finish line for the last seventy years. I stride past the crowds, trying to look as purposeful and fearless as he does, biting down on my anxiety and flooding my mouth with sudden, salty blood.

I never thought of myself as monstrous before I came here – I'm tall, but I'm proportional. Now I am a huge, pale hulk I drag around. I didn't know how blanched and fleshy I was until I saw myself in a bathhouse for the first time, white and blubbery next to lithe and dark bodies. I loom out of the steam menacingly; I displace the water in the hot pools as I settle my bulk. The adults pretend I am not there, but the small children stare at my large rubbery breasts, each as big as a baby's head, and my thatch of improbably colorful pubic hair. Somehow, like a monster, I can no longer trust this body to do my bidding – it has become strange to me, ungoverned. It has not betrayed me yet, but I'm afraid it is only a matter of time before my appendages decide to take things, literally, into their own hands.

All around me, the stands that line the busy narrow walkways stretch out baited hooks to trap me. Anime sigils blink off every gleaming surface, crawl off the signs towards me, luridly flash things I can't identify, and couldn't possibly need. My eyes down, I keep my hands rigid inside my coat sleeves. If I don't have 100% of my attention focused fiercely on them, they might sneak out of my pockets and start to rifle slyly through the stalls that crowd along the gallery; amassing secret little trinkets I don't even want about my person and then feign innocence behind my back when someone looks at me twice.

Oh, I've heard the tales. Foreigners move here, and months later, they are sent home in disgrace –caught with an illicit booty of dried squid snacks or manga comics they can't read. It's not about the haul, the thrill then, the adrenaline rush of stealing? I don't think so. It's as if they think their own mutant otherness makes them invisible. The eyes that never make contact, tricked into thinking that those gazes that slide away in the metro don't actually see them, confuse them. The simplicity of "because I can" becomes an irresistible pull – a defiant shout against every time you are shut out, ignored or simply feel confused, alone, and homesick. I can see how it will happen to me. I imagine my sneaking hands, the meaningless objects turned out of my pockets, the police car in front of the school, my students whispering behind their books. I see myself suddenly all too visible standing before the board of education, my *gaijin* eyes fixed on the gluey carpet while my boss drones about shame and face.

I wouldn't be downtown now risking my rogue fingers if I could help it. I order everything online now. I haven't been to as much as a supermarket in months. But my mother has thrown me in harm's way. Last summer when she visited me, she saw the most darling tea set in the posh Takashimaya department store. At the time, she resisted the outrageous prices, but now she regrets it. I have been given a mission from mum and the tea set must come home, wrapped in Takashimaya paper, in a Takashimaya bag, so she can show it off to her friends.

I can't say no. I can't say "sorry mum, but since you were here I seem to have gone crazy. Sorry mum, but I'm terrified my hands are going to steal something on their own."

When I was a child, my mother would scold me for my creeping hands, those unconscious childhood habits: thumb-sucking, nose-picking, fingernail biting, down to the ragged edges of skin. "Do you know where your hands have been?" she would ask in horror. I imagined my hands, crawling off on their own to dance along germ-infested railway seats and caress toilet door handles. Once, when I was barely eight, she told me that Jesus could see what my hands did under the bed sheets at night. On Sundays I would sit rigid in church under his plaster glare and wonder, what my hands might do that God would disapprove of. I wondered if they'd already done it and I hoped Jesus didn't mind. Oh, all the trouble your hands could get you into!

I guess you think I sound crazy. My bet is if you think hard, really think, you'll remember an occasion it happened to you, a time your Judas hands got you in trouble. Maybe that time in the Uffizi, when you couldn't resist the smooth, alabaster beauty of some Apollo – didn't even know you'd reached out a reverent hand to caress the marble until the security guard reprimanded you, your greasy fingers near a Michelangelo. Or maybe you're the kind who can be provoked, some child - yours or someone else's - insolently defying you until your hand twitched, flashed out, and slapped with your brain ten seconds behind screaming not to do it. Maybe you're the perv on the crowded train, who watches in horrified disbelief as his stubby fingers reach out to pinch a nipple, grope a behind, or take an upskirt shot. Or maybe not. Maybe it's just me.

Somehow I've pushed through the post-work hustle and I'm on the threshold of Takashimaya. The ground floor seethes with perfumes, an endurance course of tiny bottles and easily concealable items. In some remote part of my brain, I register my physical symptoms – wheezing breaths and heart squeezed in my chest like my body is two sizes too small.

Ironically, my mental health has improved, if I look at the macro-level. All those little overwhelming anxieties I used to be prey to have disappeared. I was always so afraid that I would get off at the wrong station or catch the wrong train completely. I was always irritatingly early for everything, so worried I would be late, miss my flight, my appointment, my friend. Here my little neuroses were tripled, quadrupled – afraid of the wrong motorway turn, afraid of saying the wrong thing in Japanese, making some huge cultural faux pas. Now, I am so consumed by the idea of shoplifting, by the phobia that my hands will take on a life of their own, that all my other fears have vanished.

I freeze in the doorway buffeted by unflinching crowds of shoppers and tourists. Behind me, someone grunts as they are pushed into me, then another person into them. The weight of the crowd propels me forward and shoots me out like a champagne cork. I find myself at the foot of the escalator and stumble onto it. I dig my hands deep into my pockets and grasp the satiny lining – I will not take them out until I need to pick the teapot off the shelf and take it to the cash register. I will not make room in these pockets for any strays.

I wish I hadn't worn my winter jacket. It is large on me and feels like I could easily stash several items under it. There is a shop girl on the home goods floor and I feel her staring at me, calculating what might be hidden under the roomy folds. She startles me with a loud accusatory welcome "Irrashaimase!" I jump slightly, then feel foolish; she is not even looking at me, parroting her greeting every half minute or so to any customer in a ten meter radius.

Maybe they won't have the teapot anymore! "Sorry mum, all sold out," I will say. "Nothing else was as nice." But there it is a pretty, stylized wave pattern in indigo blue with a bamboo handle and matching cups. I pretend I am looking at the price, then, that I am deliberating between it and its

184

neighbor. But in reality, I cannot take my hands out of my pockets. They have gone numb from grasping my coat lining and I cannot unclasp them.

I look down, as if visual contact might loosen them, and instead I see my gloves sticking up, like burgundy fingers ready to creep out of my pockets. I glance helplessly towards the shop girl to see if she has spotted their potential for Frankenstein movement. Has she seen my heavy breathing and fixed stare? I hope that she will think I'm high instead of crazy, just some strung out foreigner.

I shove the gloves deep in my pockets. The sudden motion upsets the teapot and I quickly steady it. The shop girl starts and really stares at me and then comes toward me with a hesitant smile on her face. She is marshalling her best English. I imagine for a brief, sweet moment that I will point to the teapot, she will pick it up for me; we will go to the register together, chatting in my beginner's Japanese. She will giggle shyly at my accent. But my body is flooding with sickening adrenaline flashes. The teapot lurks on the shelf like a scorpion and not all the calm, rational logic in the world can make my heart rate slow. *My hands simply will not move.*

It is too much – I turn and flee, back down the escalator, through the perfumes and make up and out the door running, bumping the browsers and the gawkers. I hear a voice yell "oi!"

185

behind me, but I am gone, weaving and ducking between the people in the streets, desperately obvious, my foreign camouflage gone.

Past a teashop, a teriyaki restaurant, through little old world streets in a part of Osaka I do not know. A haven beyond guidebook entries, the shops sell indigo-dyed door curtains, artfully clumsy tea bowls and antique step chests. I half glance around for the film extras - a Samurai emerging from a cheap NHK set, or an improbable Geisha practicing her lines. Instead, I nearly knock over a little toothless grandmother. My invisibility cloak is long gone and she smiles at me, bent double in her drab greys and greens and tells me to slow down. It astonishes me that she speaks to me, that my Hulkish monstrousness is obscured. Can't she see that I am a freakish person, a risk to commerce, to law, to tranquility? She thinks I am simply a person, running too fast in these narrow, bicycle-filled lanes.

I reach a station and stop, panting. It's not the station I meant to go to – I cannot even read the name, but I duck inside – it will take me somewhere. I cannot feel my fingers, they are numb, no longer mine at all. I hold them in front of me as I climb the stairs to the elevated platform, staring at these strange, white starfish on the ends of my arms. That is when I realize there is something gripped in my right hand, my fingers clasped tightly around it. I turn the hand over and pry the

186

fingers open. On my palm sits a blue and white ceramic circle. I cannot even identify it at first, but then I realize it is a chopstick rest, part of a set of five that sat next to my mother's teapot.

My hands are shaking uncontrollably now just like the rest of my body. I am sure that everyone in the station is staring at me from the corner of their eyes. The chopstick rest clatters from my hand to the platform and I do not stoop to pick it up. An express train is coming, rattling the lines in time with my quivering hands, about to rush through at bullet-train speeds on its way to more important places. A phrase suddenly comes to me, from a childhood of churchgoing, as clear as if I had heard it spoken aloud. *"And if thy right hand offend thee..."* Matthew 5:30. I repeat it to myself, astounded at the clarity of it, at the aptness. *"And if thy right hand offend thee..."* I walk to the platform edge. Not where the train rounds the curve and you have to "mind the gap between platform and train", but where it straightens and runs close to the concrete. I can hear the train coming; hear the overhead speaker with its monotonous "Go-chui kudasai, go-chui kudasai," warning people to stand back. *"...cut it off and cast it from thee."* I kneel down and hold my hands over the edge of the platform, and wait for the train to come.

LUCID DREAMING

By Val Muller

*L*ucid dreaming was Betsy Wylde's escape from hum-drum life. She'd taught Latin for thirty years and there wasn't much she hadn't seen. Despite the variety of teenage behavior she daily encountered, conjugating verbs just didn't hold the thrill it once did. The job was a far cry from her early days when she fought nightmares of forgetting to plan a lesson, or marking a quiz with the wrong answer key, or offending a student, or coming to school half-naked. She'd always feared losing control of a situation, but thirty years in, there was little she couldn't control. With nothing to fear, life became a dreary chore.

But lucid dreaming—ever since she saw the documentary about it—held the promise of new experiences. The documentary had been created to help people overcome nightmares, but Betsy had been practicing the technique for just the opposite reason: to pursue them.

Many weeks of effort culminated in her first lucid moment. In a dream, she had been driving toward the beach when she consciously turned the steering wheel to drive instead to the mountains. It was a pointless decision, irrelevant other than the fact that it was a decision.

She went to school that day with a bounce in her step. She postponed her killer etymology quiz (to her students' delight). She even greeted Principal Richards (who she usually went out of her way to avoid that SOB). She took the stairs instead of the elevator and she walked the long way—through the science wing—to her car. She wanted to tire herself out to fall asleep all the sooner.

***

The second lucid dream was a bit more intense. She was standing on stage, and she felt terribly anxious.

"Come on, Ms. Wylde," cried a voice from the audience. "We're all waiting to watch you perform." She glared out into the darkened auditorium, looking for the source of the voice, which she knew to be Principal Richards'. Betsy could hear shuffling and murmuring around him and she knew he had gathered the rest of the staff of Hartsbury High School to watch her. She hated them all, those cheerful do-gooders. No way would she perform for them like this, not even in a dream. She tried to turn on the lights with her mind, but it was too complicated a task. She settled instead on forcing the curtain to close, forming a heavy velvet barrier between herself and the undesirables in the audience.

If only she could do such things in her waking life.

***

She read an article by a lucid dreamer encouraging dreamers to strive to experience all five senses. She made it her goal to smell something in a dream. This time her dream started in the classroom. All of her most obnoxious students were there. Brent was sitting there in the front row with his baseball cap turned backwards and popping his gum. Max from five years ago, was snapping pictures of quizzes with his cell phone. Sherri from last year, a glowing cell phone on her lap, fingers flying and eyes wide and stupid. Yes, they were all there. Those miserable students, none of them interested in word roots, all of them obnoxious and privileged. And Ms. Wylde stood before them expected to teach. Expected to work miracles when the parents could not. The familiar tightening of her stomach warned her that her body would once again succumb to the stress of her job.

"Not again!" she said - aloud in her dream.

The class nodded. An encouragement.

"Not again!" she said more loudly. She stepped toward Max. He smelled of sweat and lust. Sherri smelled of strawberry shampoo. But it wasn't enough. To be truly lucid, she had to smell what wasn't there. She opened a literature textbook. It landed on the Exodus to *Oedipus Rex*. She never enjoyed that play, so she stared at the page until it turned to the Prologue to *The Canterbury Tales*—her favorite—instead. She blinked once more to change the modern English to Chaucer's original Middle English text. She was getting the hang of this now. She looked up to see if her students noticed. They watched her blankly.

"Well—applaud," she commanded. And the class applauded.

She smiled and bowed. Then she stood upright for her final task. She stuck her nose in her book inhaling the familiar scent of old pages. She concentrated. *Steak*, she thought. *Sizzling, seasoned, succulent steak*. She inhaled once more, and the book no longer smelled of knowledge.

"Taste," she told the class, which was already applauding again. She carried the book to them the way a waitress carries a tray and they all inhaled, licking their lips. Max took a bite first, plucking off a chunk of the text and popping it into his mouth. Instantly his face cringed and he ran to the trashcan. "Cigarette butts and vomit!" he cried.

Ms. Wylde laughed in delight. Then she carried the tray to Sherri who looked worried. "Your turn," she sang as if assigning a sentence diagram for the board.

Sherri reached for a cluster of words, which she popped into her mouth. She chewed, tears in her eyes. Swallowed. Dry heaved twice. "Roadkill," Sherri whispered. Ms. Wylde squealed and smiled. Sherri was a vegetarian.

Ms. Wylde looked down at her book and plucked out the first line of text. It tasted just the way she wanted it to—like brownie fudge batter—as sweet as the words of Chaucer himself.

***

Ms. Wylde's success in lucid dreaming improved her relations with the waking world. Fewer students misbehaved. Their teenage angst, which previously fed on Ms. Wylde's own anxiety and anger, starved during her class. She developed a bounce in her step. She smiled on a daily basis now.

In early April, Ms. Wylde entered the teacher workroom to check her mail. A gaggle of teachers greeted her.

"Good morning, Betsy!" chirped Melanie Lewis, the biology teacher. "You're looking happy these days. What's your secret?"

"Yes, we were just talking about you. We can practically feel the energy radiating from you today," added Ben Chandley, the reading specialist.

Ms. Wylde glanced out the window at the flowering pear tree swarming with bees. "Oh, just a little spring fever," she said, smiling. She stayed in the mailroom a while after the others left. Her eyes stuck on the trees; her lips curled in a smile.

She was thinking that in her dream, she'd like to climb the tree naked and let all the bees sting her flesh everywhere. Though she was terribly allergic, that didn't matter: in dreams, she could never die.

***

Ms. Wylde had to laugh at herself. One morning, Albert Berdman was being a brat. He kept turning around to talk to Susan Howard (and no wonder, with those skimpy shorts she was wearing—what happened to the enforcement of dress codes, anyway?). After telling him for the third time to turn around and focus, Ms. Wylde smirked. She raised her hands in the air and considered what sort of reptile to turn him into.

"Alakazam!" she screeched.

The class looked at her, a wide-eyed mix of shock, horror, and amusement.

Ms. Wylde looked at Albert, confounded. Why hadn't he turned into a blue tree toad? It was only when the class dissolved into heated chatter that she remembered—this was real life, not a dream. She had no power over others in real life. She checked the clock and calculated the hours until bedtime, reminding herself that she'd have to be more careful. The class continued to watch her skeptically for the rest of the period, and while she eyed them back, she bit her tongue to stifle her embarrassment. No matter. They would die in her dreams tonight. In horrible, clever ways, she would kill them all.

***

From then on, she began each dream with an amazing feat. Something to check for sure whether she was actually dreaming. She made it rain sprinkles before she travelled to her childhood home and burned the house of her obnoxious former neighbors. She turned the ocean to glitter before strapping a naked Principal Richards to a lifeguard chair, placing jellyfish on his privates, and then sending the chair into the glittery sea where the man was consumed by the Loch Ness Monster. The monster belched out the man's left hand, which Ms. Wylde stripped to bones and fashioned into a necklace that she wore for the rest of the dream.

She turned the sky tie-dyed before having sex with celebrities—most of whom she murdered in clever ways afterwards by drowning them in piles of their own money, sending them to flaming car wrecks, or—her favorite—turning into a giant praying mantis and biting off their heads.

Before long, though, she realized the more whimsical dreams bored her. The realistic ones kept just enough of the real world to thrill and excite her, so she focused on manipulating her dreams within the boundaries of realism. It made her waking hours all the more enjoyable; she spent the time looking around the ordered world and imagined how she could make it chaotic in her dreams. Still, the tedium of life, and her job, and the morons she had to work with drained her spirit to its core.

She went to bed in a stormy mood and decided she'd dream of nothing but violence and destruction. When she woke in her dream, it was morning and it was storming. She nodded at her window in approval, congratulating herself on her choice of deep purple clouds and rumbling thunder. She was almost certain this was a dream, but she had to be sure, so she hurried down the hall and turned on the washing machine glaring at it to comply. Only when it overfilled, the water rushing down the sides and seeping into the carpet of the third-floor hallway was she convinced for sure.

While waiting for the deluge, she went downstairs to the kitchen to dine completely naked. She brought a washcloth and a bottle of shampoo, setting it on the counter for later. She was listening to the washer and chowing down on graham crackers dipped in a can of chocolate frosting—diet be damned, this was a dream!—when the water from overflowing from above seeped through the ceiling enough to start a slow trickle into the dining room. Soon it became a loud enough trickle to drown out the rain outside.

Mrs. Wylde chuckled and reached for the kitchen radio. She wanted it to play "Dancing Queen." It did. She grabbed her shampoo bottle and hurried to the trickle that was quickly becoming a shower. The washing machine was flooding warm water from above. She stood on the dining room table and became the dancing queen, there, naked, dancing, showering in the deluge. As she washed her hair, the soapsuds splashed onto the dining room hardwoods and she thought with glee about the care she'd taken over the years to keep the floors pristine and gleaning.

What a thrill it was to ruin all that.

She thought briefly about causing the ceiling to collapse on her with the weight of the water—it was only a dream, after all—but she decided instead that it was time to go to school. She felt like murdering someone. Though with the darkness outside it might as well still be midnight, Ms. Wylde decided it was time to socialize. She was going to egg the other teachers' cars. Hell, why just their cars? Why not egg the teachers, too? She took her box of eighteen eggs—and a steak knife, for good measure—and put on her trench coat hanging near the door. No need to fully dress in a dream. She rather liked running around naked and the trench coat was simply badass.

She unlocked her car and prepared to get in and speed off to school, but a neighbor kid was out getting the paper. It was Little Johnny Peters, the same brat that used to play in her flowerbeds. When he saw Ms. Wylde cackling with the carton of eggs in her hand, he stared, wide-eyed. Ms. Wylde looked down to see that her trench coat wasn't closed and little Johnny was looking at her womanhood in all its glory. The boy sniffled a little. His lips trembled.

"Little fucker," she cackled, pulling the coat open all the way and jumping up and down to let every part of her drooping body jiggle for the boy.

He squealed before dropping the newspaper and rushed inside.

Still laughing, Ms. Wylde opened her car door and placed the carton of eggs inside but something worried her. Just nagging anxiety, but still—she wanted to make sure it was still a dream. She opened her garage door and retrieved her axe. She'd find out soon enough.

Behind her house was the natural gas hookup. Highly flammable. She knew because those bastards who built her house hadn't done the hookups right, and twice she had to call to have it repaired, the gassy smell of rotten eggs warning her of the shoddy workmanship. How many times did she half-wish the place actually *would* burn down?

With a wild laugh, she swung the axe at the gas line. It only took two tries before the familiar scent filled the air. With a nod, she jumped the fence and did the same thing to the gas line going into the home of little Johnny Peters. The line broke with a terrible *snap*. She was about to run off when a tiny face materialized in the back window. It was little Johnny himself. She put the axe behind her back and motioned for him to come out to the patio with her. She'd like him to inhale the gas fumes, if he didn't mind. She beckoned him with her finger, and sure enough, like a trained dog he came.

But the weight of the axe behind her gave her a better idea.

"Remember when you used to play in my garden?" she asked.

The boy nodded, wide-eyed, horrified.

"You used to pick apart my flowers. You beheaded the tulips," she sighed.

Johnny nodded.

"Well, kid." She hoisted the axe above her head before Johnny could even realize what was happening. "Payback's a bitch."

Johnny's mother was calling for him before his head even hit the ground. Ms. Wylde watched with delight as his body remained standing for a second or two too long. It reminded her of the headless horseman, its arms reaching out pathetically before plunging to the patio with a squishy *thud*.

198

"Johnny?" Mrs. Peters was calling.

Ms. Wylde cackled again as she saw the propane grill at the edge of the Peters' patio. She picked up the child's head from the ground, flipped open the barbeque lid, and placed the head inside. Then she turned on the knob and struck the "ignite" button.

The grill flared to action and the dripping liquids of the severed head sizzled almost immediately. The scent of rotten eggs was all about, but the natural gas didn't catch right away. Of course it waited until Ms. Wylde was safely away before erupting in an explosion that shook the Peters' house and then her own.

Laughing, she hurried back to her car and sped to school. All the lights stayed green for her and she passed the fire truck going in the opposite direction, pulling open her trench coat to flash the driver. At the elementary school, a bus was flashing its lights, about to stop, causing both lanes of traffic to halt for those coddled little brats on board, but Ms. Wylde didn't feel like stopping. Not in her dream. She had eggs to throw.

"Fuck 'em," Ms. Wylde said, squealing her tires. The bus driver gestured and beeped, but it didn't stop Betsy Wylde.

A police car on the opposite lane of traffic flashed its lights and pulled out in a U-turn in pursuit of the violator. The thrill of the chase sped her adrenaline. She wondered if she should cause herself to explode in a fiery crash. Or maybe get herself arrested for reckless driving and then escape from prison. Maybe she could fuck the officer in the back of his car and then bite his head off. Realism was good, but the praying mantis bit never got old. But then, the thought of prison was appealing too. She always wondered if it were true about prison violence and rape. All the action of this dream *was* rather stimulating. What better way to play it out than in a lucid nightmare?

No, she reminded herself. *First the eggs.* But the cop was still on her trail. "This is my dream, Pig," she shouted at the officer in her rear-view mirror. "And I say you turn into a—a— giant donut!" She blinked her eyes, but the officer was only just an officer. "I *said* a donut!" she screamed. But nothing happened. The police car was right behind her now, and it was flashing its lights insistently, the officer gesturing for her to pull over.

"Damn it," she yelled. "This is my dream." At the very announcement, the next traffic light turned red, but Ms. Wylde went right on through. "Not in my dream," she said. She looked back through the rear-view mirror. "Fall off a cliff and die," she instructed the cop. But a cliff did not appear, and the police officer remained in pursuit, still breathing and not, in fact, plummeting to his death.

Maybe she was focusing too hard on driving. She'd stop, pull over, and get out of the car. Then she'd be able to manipulate the cop. She decided she'd pull over by ramming into a fire hydrant. It exploded into a tall vertical column of water that quickly drained onto her now-crushed car. The airbag deployed and her neck and chest ached with the impact. She was losing her touch on lucid dreaming. The pain was far too intense.

The cop was now tapping on the window incessantly. But this was her dream, and she did not allow herself to be injured. She opened the door and stepped out, disoriented but unhurt.

"I said, you fucker, turn into a donut, fall off a cliff, and die."

The policeman's expression turned sour, and his eyes traveled downwards to take in the naked form under the trench coat.

"Oh, I see," she told the cop. "I guess I want to play praying mantis, eh? You familiar with the game?"

She approached the policeman and reached for his belt, but that's where he kept his gun, and in an instant, he had overpowered her. He had pressed her onto the ground. The trench coat had become dislodged and he now straddled her as she lay face down.

"Oh, so you like to play the dominant one?" she asked, though her voice sounded surprisingly startled for such a lucid dream.

"You are under arrest," the officer said, cuffing her and pulling her to her feet. Her womanhood hung out for all the world to see, the trench coat now halfway down her back and held up only by the handcuffs. A car or two passed by beeping wildly at the sight.

"You are now a praying mantis," Ms. Wylde told the officer. She cringed when he didn't turn. "A praying mantis," she repeated. "Alakazam!" Only his sad, startled eyes met her as she looked up at the darkened sky, she noticed a patch was clearing to the west and the miserable cheer of the sun started to peek through.

***

For decades, students told the story of the crazy murderer named Betsy Wylde who was once trusted to teach the town's best and brightest. It is said that the old storage room at Hartsburg High used to be her classroom and that it fell into disuse after her arrest. As for the once brilliant teacher, it was rumored that she got off with an insanity plea and spent the rest of her years in the Hartsbury Asylum at the west end of town where she loved to sleep and sleep and sleep more than any other patient they'd ever had there before.

Homeland

By Anne Wilson

"**W**hat is it Kim?" Pete looks concerned, but I don't want to talk about it. I don't ever want to talk about it, not now, not ever.

I twitch again, only slightly but visibly and my hand goes to my stomach. It feels as if I have been poked by something or accidentally knocked. The strange, unwelcome sensation makes my heart beat faster and bile rises in my throat. I swallow it back, feeling a little choked and panicky. I smell antiseptic.

"Don't worry", I say, "it's okay, it never lasts very long", but the truth is I actually think it may be getting worse.

I did visit the doctor when the feelings began. At first they kept me awake at night. The doctor decided it was caused by indigestion and gave me a prescription for antacid tablets. When that didn't work I went back and he gave me some tablets to calm my nerves and help me sleep better. They didn't work either so he gave me a stronger prescription. I think he thought I was attention seeking.

Later, sitting on the metro on the way home, I had time to think and the realization that I was on my own with this situation and always would be crystalized slowly. I read in a magazine about someone who had a phantom pregnancy. I thought maybe what I had was something similar. Hers was all inside her head, which is where mine must be too.

I decided I'd like to try a holiday, a change of air, a change of scene, maybe a change of diet. Pete and I deserved some quality time together; well he did anyway, he'd been working such long hours away from home. I booked us a cheap week in Spain. It even occurred to me that a solution to my problem might be to try to get pregnant and a holiday could be romantic. Pete would be pleased. He would take such good care of me. I bought a new dress and some sun preparations.

I change my position on the beach towel but my heart feels twisted, my stomach trembles, and the paella I have just eaten seems to shift uncomfortably feeling as if it's liquefying somewhere inside me. I sit up and move my hand involuntarily from my stomach to my chest.

Pete becomes more concerned; slips a comforting arm around my shoulders. "Have you been taking those tablets the doctor gave you, the stronger ones? You did bring them, didn't you?"

"Yes", I answer miserably, but it's a lie. I brought them but they aren't working either. They're in the bin in the hotel bathroom. I'll make sure they're hidden when we get back.

A young family from our hotel is a little further along the beach. Their baby cries out suddenly and I jump out of my skin. Pete laughs, but not unkindly. Pete would do anything for me and the simple knowledge of that adds to my unhappiness. I don't deserve him. More to the point, he doesn't deserve me.

"As soon as we get home, I'm coming to the doctors with you. You haven't been yourself since I came back from training." He smooths out our towels and offers me a bottle of water.

I shake my head and lie back down; try to relax. How could I ever have deceived him the way I did?

When I found out that my one drunken night with his best friend while Pete was away on an army training course had made me pregnant, I was absolutely horrified. How did things like this happen? By the time Pete returned, my dates would be all wrong. It couldn't be explained. I couldn't allow this situation to continue. I couldn't tell my friends or ask my parents for help and with every day that passed, I panicked more and more.

I found the telephone number of the clinic. I made an appointment for just two days later. I went on my own for the consultation and returned the following week for the termination. I wasn't sure what to take with me and felt terrified. Everything smelled of antiseptic, even the flowers in the vase on the table in the waiting room. I remember trying to wipe the streaks of mascara from under my eyes and a nurse giving me a box of tissues. I remember my hands trembling.

Afterwards I cried and cried. I felt hollow, as if they'd taken away too much of my insides. I'd never felt more alone. I didn't expect to care so much; after all if this pregnancy had continued it would have ruined my life and yet now it was over. I felt more alone than I'd ever felt. Alone and haunted by my thoughts.

Pete returned and our lives carried on as normal. His friend didn't know what had happened. What I'd been through are the rare occasions we met and he gave no sign of even remembering our drunken fling. He never gave me any reason to worry that he might tell Pete the truth.

"Shall we go back to the hotel and get ready for dinner? Don't want you to overdo the sunbathing; especially if you're feeling a bit fragile." Pete still looks worried.

"I'm okay now", I lie. I sit up and begin to gather my things together. "I think I had hiccups. You remember saying the paella had a funny taste at lunchtime? You were probably right. Let's go out to a restaurant tonight and have a change."

"Good idea," Pete says, shaking our sandy beach towels and folding them up. "You go in the bathroom first and have a long soak. You haven't worn your new dress yet; how about wearing it tonight?"

I smile and nod my head. The weird feeling has left me for now and each time it leaves, I hope desperately that it won't return. I never really thought it was caused by indigestion but I suppose it could be nerves. If only I could relax and move on from what happened, I wouldn't need to see the doctor again, wouldn't need sleeping tablets.

I retrieve my half-empty little bottle of tranquillizers out of the bathroom bin and resolve to take them again. I need all the help I can get. I take a double dose to start me off. Don't want any more dreams about phantom pregnancies.

The unfamiliar bathroom has wall to floor tiling with a sort of grey marble vein running through it. Not what I would have chosen, but I suppose it looks all right here. I wonder if all the bathrooms are exactly the same... four hundred and seventy bathrooms, with four towels in each one, two bath size, two-hand size, and a toweling bath mat. That must mean . . . how many towels . . .?

I suppose I drift off out of things a bit. The tranquillizers and the atmosphere in here is all steamy because I shut the door and the air extraction vent doesn't seem to work, it just rattles a lot.

I left Pete lying on the bed in his underpants watching a football match. Someone scores a goal, I can hear the crowd's elation and the mattress on the bed protesting as Pete bounces up and down. After a while he shouts to ask if I'm all right.

"Fine! What time is it?" I open my eyes and sit further up the bath. The feeling has come back stronger than ever. My whole body stiffens as I feel the sensation of my belly being softly nudged, very gently prodded. I look at the shiny ceramic toilet bowl in front of me and wonder if I might be sick. The smell of antiseptic is strong in here.

I look down, expecting marks to be showing on my skin somehow and imagine I see them, tiny and pale.

Then I become aware of an amorphous thing floating in the steam above my body. The edges are translucent, but slowly I see a curving core, rubbery jelly, like a grub with a large head.

My feet and legs go rigid as I try to push myself backwards up the bath, away from it. I crack my elbow against the damp tiled wall and can't suppress a sharp yelp of pain just as another goal is scored. I can hear my heartbeat and feel pressure in my chest from holding in the scream, which would bring Pete hammering on the bathroom door. I look around me wildly, fighting panic and nausea.

The thing drops downwards and bumps itself against my naked wet belly.

I am trapped in the bath with a scream trapped in my throat.

Irrational Fears

The thing nudges against me again like a glutinous, misshapen soap bubble. I can see it has two black dots for eyes and buds where the limbs would have formed; it's on the outside trying to get back in, back home.

How to Spot One

By Carol L. Park

I wasn't sure I wanted this prospective customer. My business installs and monitors household alarms. A few years back I broke from a big name company. It felt great to be an independent operator at first. I could make my own decisions and set my own hours. But then I wasted time and materials installing alarms on people I couldn't possibly continue to service. When I was one small piece of a big system, someone else made the first call on a prospective customer, offered a contract, and afterwards I installed the alarm and problem-solved any malfunctions. My work was all on regular hours. It's different when you're on your own. It was now on me to choose whom to take on and now all the complaints come to me.

I wasn't prepared for the crazies. The losses seriously ate into my pay stub, and more. My first one was Ann. Only two days after I installed a new system for her, she phoned.

"There are strange hairs on countertop! I must have had an intruder, but it didn't sound."

I went and demonstrated the alarm. It worked. Definitely no malfunction. Those hairs could have been from her cat or a friend. The second time, my friend—Teri—had pulled

her top up and over her head. It was her first time in my
bedroom. Modest, she had her back turned towards me. My
hand was poised over her pink bra strap, ready to unhook it.
Already, above Teri's low-cut jeans, I could see little bumps.
Excitement—it tingled through her and me.

Wouldn't you know—right then my business line rang:
Ann is in a frenzy. Needed me like yesterday. She wouldn't wait.
I couldn't afford to lose my reputation so early in the game. *On
my way.* I pulled on my shirt and jacket, while I apologized
profusely to Teri. That moment with her vanished.

Ann's problem turned out to be cats in heat
caterwauling near her window. I cut her contract when I could.
You see, to stay afloat you have to read the signs. Know a real
paranoid.

Months after Ann, a stranger at 912 Capgrass Court,
Apartment 307, cracked open her front door to peer at me as I
mouthed what was written on my badge: "Baily with Ward's
Alarms. Are you Kathy Reagan?"

She nodded and opened it wider.

At first, I took Kathy to be young. She looked so slim in
her halter-top and had no cleavage. But closer up, I saw the
folds on her neck giving sign of aging. Emaciated, that's what
she was. Then I saw her pale, shrunken hands. My unease grew.
She talked non-stop about security concerns while I stretched

my tape from door to corner to measure, then on to the next. No need to sell on this one.

In a voice both thin and frail, she told a story of two guys harassing her. They'd been neighbors at a previous apartment and though she moved to escaped them, they followed. "All that matters is keeping them out." She held one hand in another, twisting.

"That's what alarms are for."

The living room where she stood was empty except for two plastic chairs and two stacks of boxes. "They take turns watching. They lurk at the creek!" She moved to the far wall to pull back a black sheet, which covered a balcony entrance. Beyond it lay a gully and trees. "He breaks in when I go out."

Already her alarm knotted my shoulders. "You've told the police?"

"Of course, but they're too clever. They never find them."

"How do you know someone's broken in?"

"The smell! Isn't it awful?" Her cheeks and nose wrinkled up as if she inhaled skunk.

Silent, I stared. I couldn't agree.

"It's been three days. Come." At the end of a hallway, she threw open a closet door. "It's still in here!"

I peered over her at towels, an iron, and bottles of cleaners, and then shrugged. Close up to her now, I could see the red splotching her hands. A sign—much terror, too often.

"Can't you smell him?"

Only stale air, trapped too long inside. "No, sorry mam." Politeness is policy. My eyes darted to the nearby bathroom. Scads of gloves draped the sink—what I'd also seen in the kitchen. "The gloves?"

"They keep coming in when I leave, so I have to clean."

She took from the closet a towel, scrunched it, and held it to my nose. "Smell it?"

I stepped back. "Can't say I do."

A whack job for sure. Her eyes pulled at me. Frenzied, like a pool ball spinning in a socket. I wanted to help her, but an alarm wouldn't do it.

"He rubs my towels there!" She thrust the towel in front of my crotch and circled it 'round.

I wanted to speed on out and leave off politic good-byes, but I did it right. "Sorry, I've got to go."

"A contract—you'll send it?"

"In a few." Wished I could send a doctor.

"And after I send it off, how long until the alarm's set up?"

"It's a busy time. Not sure."

Her shallow chest folded in. "I'd better buy a gun."

My lie fell heavy on my shoulders. What else would follow?

I said my thanks and goodbye and while my eyes studied the stairs I went down, my mind searched my contact list. It was no use. No one I knew would help her. No forcing her to a shrink.

I climbed in my truck and looked up towards Kathy's apartment. She stood watching, so thin, so scared. I needed my mantra.

I'm an alarm man, nothing more, I repeated. I even sang it aloud as I drove down streets looking for people who held a cell phone or, better yet, the hand of their child or partner, instead of wringing their hands together. People with more than skin on their bodies. People looking wonderfully normal.

Yet since that visit, more than once Kathy has appeared before me—her emaciated body and hands looking bleached, fingers interlocked as she twists them round and round. Worst: the headline: "Delivery man shot at Capgrass Court." An alarm that keeps sounding.

Meet the authors...

Essel Pratt is the Author of Final Reverie and ABC's of Zombie Friendship. He currently appears in over thirty anthologies. Essel holds an Associates of Arts in Psychology and is working towards a Bachelors of Science. Essel focuses his writing on horror, while intertwining fantasy within.

Wayne Via lives in Dana Point, California with his wife Pam. To find a complete list of the anthologizes that include short stories by Wayne, please go to waynevia.com.

Lance Hyden was born in the mean no, high-spirited streets of Detroit, Michigan. He traded the cold for heat by moving to Phoenix, Arizona during high school. After being stationed in California while serving in the Marine Corp, Lance moved back to Michigan and graduated from Eastern Michigan University with a degree in film. Finding the sun more attractive than the snow, Lance moved back to Arizona where he lives with his girlfriend and their 4 boys.

Katherine Hannula Hill is a contributing writer for Spirit magazine and the writer and content editor for the Kelly Ann

Brown Foundation of Marin Community Foundation's website. Her short story "Ella" was recently chosen for an anthology to be published by Zimbell House Publishing.

After years of considering himself a writer, **Paul Rhodes** decided that it was time to stop scribbling on beer mats and cocktail napkins and get serious. His short story "Death of a Cockroach" was shortlisted in Writer's Monthly Magazine. He lives in Faversham, England with his wife, Faye, and son, Dylan.

Matthew Lett currently resides in Tulsa, OK. Having written for many years, a list of his publishing credits include books/anthologies in both paperback and e-format with Wolf on Water Publishing, Books to Go Now, and Noodle Doodle Publications, to name a few.

Tracey Chapman is a stay at home mum only working part time as a taxi driver. She is currently doing taken writing courses to hone her craft. Spectrophobia is her first piece of published work.

DJ Tyrer is the person behind *Atlantean Publishing* and has been widely published in anthologies and magazines around the world, including *Amok!* (April Moon Books) and *State of Horror: Illinois* (Charon Coin Press), and has a novella available in paperback and on the Kindle, *The Yellow House* (Dynatox Ministries).

Alex Harasymiw actively writes fiction in his time off from work as a freelance, technical translator. Based out of Newmarket, Ontario, his work has appeared in *Sulphur: Laurentian University's Literary Journal* (2011-15), *ArtAscent*'s "Hidden" and forthcoming, "Portrait" themed showcases (2014-15), and *Chupa Cabra House*'s "Small Town Futures" anthology (2014), among others. Links to some of his work can be found on his blog: http://amharasymiw.wordpress.com/about/

The Other Side of the Door author **David Bergheim** draws inspiration from different literary genres in his offbeat works of fiction. His first novel, Greenbeaux – about a clown running for president – received critical acclaim from Kirkus Review. Bergheim studied English Literature at the University of Arizona and has an MBA from Yale.

John Timm lives with artist wife Susan amid the prickly plants, animals and humans of the Arizona High Sonoran Desert. When not writing, he teaches foreign languages and communication at a local university. His work has appeared in *Bartleby Snopes, Perspective Literary Magazine, The Story Shack* and elsewhere.

Paul Griley is a high school English teacher with 20 years of experience, having taught creative writing, literature, journalism and newspaper production class at the high school levels. Some of his previous students have since become published writers and college professors.

Robin Becker is the rambling type, having lived on both coasts as well as several fly-over zones. She currently teaches creative writing at Minnesota State University. Her first novel, Brains: A Zombie Memoir, was published by Harper Collins and she is hard at work on the next.

Living in Northern California, and writing under the pen name of **Thomas Elson** has a recent short story, *Mandamus,* which appeared in the *Clackamas Literary Review.*

Casey Douglass has been writing dark and horror fiction for a number of years as well as pursuing other word-based goals. A self-identified bleak geek, he is slowly molding his writing into a shape and form that pleases himself and hopefully, the people that read it.

Erin O'Loughlin has lived and worked in Australia, Japan, Italy and Germany as an editor, writer and teacher. She has edited books and academic papers, translated books from Italian to English, and co-authored academic papers, but her secret real love is writing fiction.

Val Muller is an author and teacher living in Virginia. Inspired by her dogs, she pens the kidlit mystery series Corgi Capers and is also the author of the YA novel The Scarred Letter and the supernatural chiller Faulkner's Apprentice with several novels forthcoming. You can find out more at www.ValMuller.com.

Anne Wilson's short fiction has appeared in various anthologies; most recently *Light in the Dark* from Bridge House Publishing. Living in Mallorca inspired her first novel, *Here Be Dragons: A Tale of Mortals, Myths and Mystery*, set there and in Denmark. Current projects are another novel and a sequel to *Dragons*.

Exploring geographies—physical and internal—is **Carol L. Park's** pursuit in writing and life. It has taken her to Tokyo where she conversed in Japanese and taught English as well. The last decade, California has been her home where she writes of actual experiences and fiction. A novel set in Tokyo is under revision.

Irrational Fears

Irrational Fears